# RSVP: A NOVEL

**RUCHIRA KHANNA**

In Memory of my Parents

&

To all those individuals who are stuck with their past. May
you be mindful to the call of the universe and live what
the present has to offer.

# Contents

# Contents

# Acknowledgements

I am deeply thankful to all the people who supported me while I wrote this book.

A special thanks to my husband who always encourages and supports my writing. Thank you for believing in my work.

A big shout out to Sumana Khan for her 2 cents.

Charli Mills – your help and support are peerless, as always!

# CHAPTER ONE

*"To live is the rarest thing in the world. Most people exist, that is all."* — **Oscar Wilde**

*Splash!*

*There is a strange tranquility as I realize I am surrounded by endless blue fluid. I try to talk, but no voice comes out. I frantically try looking around but except for the infinite azure, I cannot see anything.*

*With clenched fists, eyes wide open, and mouth shut tightly, I'm trying hard to understand where I am. I faintly remember having wished to be unborn, floating aimlessly in Ma's womb. Has that wish come true?*

*That's when I briefly catch a glimpse of Yogi. Oh no! We're drowning. I begin flapping my hands to stay afloat. I rise, only to be sucked inside again. My hands are now paining. I cannot do it anymore.*

*Gasp!*

**********

Jay woke up with a jerk, breathing hard, sweaty with his hands flayed up mid-air. The nightmare felt real, and he thought he was going to die. His hands went to his throat inadvertently remembering that choking feeling. Recollecting his psychologist, Susan's suggestion, he tried taking deep breaths. His sudden action made Yogi also rise with a woof, making him quickly jump from his sofa dog bed and get cozy next to his master.

Jay was quick to hug him, all the while taking deep breaths to return to normalcy. His eyes were twitching with droplets of sweat forming around his forehead. Licking his dry lips, he gulped imaginary spittle to moisten his parched throat, the image of him drowning simply refusing to leave his mind. "Susan mentioned this would go away. Alas! When? Why does this *same* nightmare haunt me? And whose voice is this?" Jay mumbled.

He paused for a breather, wiping the sweat off his forehead with the back of his arm while continuously patting his pet in a futile attempt to console himself. "Why? Why?" he moaned, trying to blink his moist, heavy eyes while attempting to reason out but no luck. The night-light was flashing various colors. He kept glancing at it for a sign, but no clarification came to him. His bedroom wore a scanty look equipped with just a queen-size bed and a table on each side that stood empty with no pictures.

He glanced at the clock that was beaming three in the morning on his side table. "Gosh! Another two hours of sleep, and slumber now refuses to take over," he moaned. As if on the cue, Yogi began to lick his cheeks trying to relax his master.

Jay lay with the dog over him, allowing Yogi to soothe his fraying nerves, and soon he drifted off to la-la land. A couple of hours later, the alarm woke Yogi and him up with a startle. They stared at each other. Jay was embarrassed at first to see Yogi by his side as he remembered his nightmare. Sitting up on the bed with a jolt, he kept pressing the temples of his forehead while walking toward the bathroom, leaving Yogi puzzled since he hadn't received any cuddles from his master yet.

"Atta boy!" he ordered stepping out of the room dressed and wearing his running shoes. Jay leashed his pup, and the duo was out to catch some fresh air. Once back home, he was deep in thought while working monotonously. In a state of daze after crushing the coffee beans, he plugged in the coffee maker. Yogi was quick to break his chain of thoughts with a *woof.*

Jay acknowledged Yogi's woof with a nod and smile, but that did not deter him. Finally, he bent down to stroke his fur which brought satisfaction to this small, compact, and hardy beagle as his hazel eyes and soft pleading expression made Jay melt with guilt over his earlier actions. A chuckle by Jay broke the silence, and Yogi's tactics went berserk. "How can I ever be thankful enough to you?" he admitted while stroking both his ears playfully. "You are gentle, sweet, and so friendly that it has brought me out of the funk I was in!"

He poured Yogi's dry food in his bowl and went for a quick shower. Yogi could not be disturbed. He was busy gobbling up his first meal of the day. While dressing, Jay remembered his three o'clock dream and paused while pressing his fingers on the teeth of his comb. He stared into the mirror with his gullible, deep-set eyes that were the window to all the memories he has made for the last twenty-seven years which provided those deep, visible lines on his forehead.

*The mirror was rewinding the dream.*

Sleepless nights, headaches, muscle cramps, and low back pain were a norm until he met Susan, his therapist. Thankfully, the pain was gone, but the occasional sleepless nights tormented him every time he delved into his past. It would bring back those memories he still could not triumph over, and he was adamant to keep the past in the past. Anyone who would try to bring those memories to the forefront would be chastised.

*Woof.*

*Woof.*

That sound made him come out of his reverie.

"Yes... yes... I'm coming."

Jay was appreciative of Yogi since his pet could always feel his emotions whenever he was lost, upset, or low. He quickly combed his hair before bending down to stroke Yogi's smooth white and tan fur. "Atta boy!" Walking toward the kitchen, he opened the door to the backyard so that his pet could relieve himself while he grabbed his freshly brewed cup of coffee.

As he sat on a chair, he noticed the empty bowl and eyed his puppy. Bladder empty, the pet was quick to place his two front paws on his leg and began his ritual of licking his face.

"No! Not the face, Yogi," Jay objected as he pulled his face away, then paused to contemplate and gushed with embarrassment. "I am an opportunist, right?" Yogi paused and twisted his head sideways as if trying to decipher that word. For him, Jay was his dad, his caretaker, and he was obliged to take care of him whenever any opportunity arose. The word *opportunist* was a vague unit of language for him.

"Come on, buddy. Let's go earn some money, so we can fulfill that bucket list of ours," said Jay, opening the door for his pet.

# CHAPTER TWO

*"Life is what happens to us while we are making other plans."*
— **Allen Saunders**

"Oh, stop it. Not the face. Stop it," Jay Sethi pleaded all the while grinning, fussing, and pulling his face away to wipe it with his long-sleeve shirt.

"How many times have I told you... *not* the face," he said with a firm and deep voice. Just then, the light turned green, and Jay resumed driving as he rolled down the window. The passenger wallowed, whimpered for a bit, then settled down when he realized his master was serious. He looked at him with his puppy eyes to which Jay gave a quick look, but it was a flinty expression encouraging Yogi to fuss a bit before covering his face with his paw.

The early Monday morning breeze was crisp and chilly, but it was captivating to the senses. Jay inhaled deeply, allowing all his senses to fill with the elixir of life. The altocumulus clouds had enveloped the sky indicating precipitation, but the winds were shifting gears now and then, leading to a prediction of drought this year by the meteorologists. His black hair ruffled in the light wind showing off his receding hairline that he had combed just before leaving his two-bedroom, two-bath townhome. As the horizontal wrinkles on his forehead smoothed with the gentle breeze wiping all his worries temporarilyaway, he felt energized. Soon, his right hand went toward the passenger seat. "How can I stay angry at you?" he said in an amused tone.

A quick lick, adoration, and muffled voice made Jay's full lips part and show his pearly whites with tiny dimples appearing at the corner of his mouth accentuating his chiseled jawline. Soon, the car turned into a shopping complex on Homestead Road in Los Altos Hills, California. Brakes screeched and the hand brake was pulled. He glanced at the neon board that displayed 'Got T' andsmirked over it with pride while stepping out of his 2001 Toyota Corolla, leaving his door ajar for his pet. Yogi jumped onto the street and woofed, which was an indication for his owner to pick him up. He shut the door behind him and pressed the remote. It gave off an audible noise that echoed far and near as the white clouds were scudding across the blue sky at six o'clock on an early October morning.

Jay bent his six-foot frame to pick up his buddy who was adopted from the shelter exactly sixteen months ago with the hope and intention of helping him heal. His therapist had prescribed this, adding that pets are known to be stressbusters. Alas! There are still some nights that are restless and antsy which he spends tossing and turning.

Jay walked with steady steps toward his store, holding his pet and ruffling his ears. The two-year-old beagle woofed as Jay deactivated the alarm before entering the store. Jay swung the door open, making Yogi jump off and race toward his sofa dog bed. He pounced on it and after swirling around for a bit, settled in. Getting up early had never been his favorite time of the day, but his master's job demanded it. Nevertheless, he began his day with a treat that would excite him resulting in him licking Jay's face despite loads of fuss and groans from his master. Yogi was complacent in these surroundings since he knew all the friendly faces and hands that would greet and pet him.

Turning on the fluorescent lights, Jay grinned at the scenario and adjusted the thermostat to seventy degrees Fahrenheit while shutting down the dimmers. He opened the faux wood blinds covering two large windows. The walls were paneled in wood to shoulder height. There was a big blackboard hanging between the two windows. The decor consisted of maple-colored chairs and tables with a full-wall mural of a redwood forest.

Lastly, he walked toward the counter, turned on a lamp, and hummed a prayer. That was one ritual he had carried from his home in India since it grounded him while giving him a certain hope and peace within to start a new day full of possibilities.

After a few moments of reverie, he started getting on with the chores—removing five-gallon jugs of flavored iced tea and pre-made food from the refrigerator, turning on the oven for the eats that were pre-prepared the night before, and crushing various condiments such as ginger, cardamom, and mint in individual Black and Decker blender jars. Turning on the gas stove, he placed three ten-gallon stainless steel stockpots on the burners, which had water and tea leaves in them. While removing gallons of one percent, two percent, and nonfat milk from the huge refrigerator, he was eyeing the clock on the wall waiting for his first customer, Ronald, to arrive. Ronald was none other than the delivery guy of his customized tableware supplies that were delivered every month. Just when the oven beeped with the set temperature, the door chimed followed by a woof from Yogi. Jay was quick to turn around.

"Hey! Good morning," came an announcement.

"Your ginger tea with milk will be ready in a bit," Jay announced, adding the condiments to each of the boiling stockpots.

"Aye, man. No rush. I make my delivery early to you so that I can enjoy that special cup before I actually start my regular route," Ronald said pushing his handcart into the store that had five twelve-inch boxes on it. Being the usual delivery guy ever since Jay started his business, he knew his way around the stockroom. After unloading the cargo, he played with Yogi until he got a whiff of his beverage. Jay put a bowl of water next to his pet and sat across from Ronald with his cup of tea.

"I'm assuming business is booming since I saw the increase in the merchandise orders from three to five cartons for a month's supply," stated Ronald in between a few sips of the scalding tea.

"Quite good, actually. I might just get close to crossing out one of my bucket list items in about... umm, one month's time," said Jay with a confident tone, pulling out some Parle-G wheat biscuits and honey crackers from a cookie jar.

"That is neat, man," exclaimed Ronald and stood up to high-five the owner which he was quick to return.

"Three years into this business, and you have put your heart and soul into it," Ronald exclaimed with pride, biting into the cookie. "Although, I must admit when I first came in to deliver your goods, I was skeptical."

Jay frowned at that comment, and Ronald did not hesitate to explain, "America is all about coffee, man. Tea is a British thing. But what can I say, your unique menu got me addicted to it."

Jay was quick to smile widely, accentuating his dimples. "I have put my all in it for this success." Resting his back on the chair and crossing his leg while reminiscing, he said, "I lost quite a bit, so I had to switch gears. Fortunately, my green card came on time. I quit my corporate job, took a loan, and went back to my grass roots for stability because I was always trembling due to the breakup and the credit card pile-up," he said in an acerbic tone. "At home, tea has always been our basic beverage since I was a toddler, and I have many fond memories of it. All I did was mix and match with various condiments, advertised it with a 'Got T' label, and the rest is history."

Ronald raised his cup while nodding assertively. They continued to sip their beverages in silence. Yogi sniffed his owner's shoes for attention. That was enough to break the reticence. Jay got up to open the door for him to help him lighten his bladder.

As he stood there watching his pet doing his deed, Ronald continued, "Man, I feel for you. You got bruised wickedly, and all you wanted was stability and love."

Jay looked at him with muggy eyes. "Call it destiny." He gave out a deep sigh. "I'm hoping the bad is behind me, though," he said with a smirk. Soon the kitchen needed his attention, and he got busy. Ronald finished his beverage. The aroma from the oven made Jay walk toward it to avoid the eats getting smoldered.

"Man, the distinctive smell of spices always makes me hungry. What's baking in the oven?" asked the curious delivery guy. "I ought to stay longer for them to be done so that I can pick one of each," he humored.

Jay gave out a noticeable smile. "I have vegetarian and lamb samosas, and egg, chicken, and vegetarian puffs. Fortunately, I pre-make them the night before, so baking them the next day is an easy task." The owner gave a quick peek into the oven and approached his cash register to ring him up. "I will try to remember to keep leftovers for you a day prior to your arrival and will give you at a fifty percent discount," he said in a candid tone to which Ronald gave a quick nod.

"That will be four dollars and fifty-three cents. The cookies were on the house." The delivery guy searched for the change and was short three cents.

"No worries, you can pay me next time. We will be meeting in another twenty-eight days. Although, you are always welcome to stop by for a cup of tea. I have introduced talent night on Wednesdays, and you would love it," Jay said with a wide smile and honest expression writing down the three cents due in a notebook.

"Wow! That's so innovative." Ronald was quick to turn toward the blackboard that was hanging along the wall between the two windows. "Gosh, all your evenings are booked."

Jay was quick to correct, "Except for Sundays."

"Man, you are too ambitious," Ronald mocked.

Jay blushed and pretended to adjust the strap of his watch. "I love what I do, so why bother to take a break?"

"Also, for whom should I take a break?" he mumbled to himself.

"The schedule is the same as last time except for the addition on Wednesday. I see how you have maintained a relationship with the respective instructors to continue," Ronald praised.

Jay was quick to add, "The secret is simple. All their drinks and snacks are on the house. Although I do take a small commission from them for hosting their classes here." He smirked. "No doubt the amount I make from the orders via those customers is massive."

"Aha." The delivery guy pointed his two thumbs at him. "Bang on."

"So which book are they reading in the book club on Mondays?"

"It's chalked on the board." Jay pointed toward it, busy shelving his eats under the glass shelf.

"It's *Two by Two* by Nicholas Sparks."

"Nah! Don't have time for that, maybe next week. How can I look out for the next book?"

"Check out my website, man. I will update it according to what the book club moderator tells me."

"And there is chess night on Tuesdays. Now who in the name of thy heaven comes to play chess on a weeknight?"

"Well, teens and young adults." Jay gleamed with a twinkle and added, "In fact, I join in from time to time for a game or two depending on the traffic in the store."

"Aha. Good for you."

There was a pause as Ronald was scrutinizing the blackboard. "Wow, I would love to do this someday!" he remarked with lots of energy.

"Painting night, huh?"

Jay added, "I have a waiting list for this one. Would you like me to add your name to it?"

"Sure, man."

Jay removed his vinyl gloves and opened another diary, which was entitled, 'Painting Night.'

"There is a ten-dollar deposit, please," he added.

"Seriously?"

"Yup! This is to confirm you will show up when your painting night approaches. This deposit will go toward your painting expenses." He paused, then continued, "By the way, this policy of taking the deposit is not my idea. It's the painter who conducts the class who insisted on this. I just earn a small commission," he said in an earnest tone.

"Oh! That's okay, man. I trust you. But what if I am out of town or something?"

"Diana gives you two Thursday options. You can choose either one of them. Believe me she is quite flexible, and I have never had issues with any customers," he said with confidence that made Ronald quickly hand him the ten-dollar bill.

While Jay was scribbling his details, the delivery guy gave out a loud chuckle. "Boy, Fridays would be a chick pick-up night."

"Well, not exactly. Stress can do numbers on even the men these days," Jay pointed out as he gave a quick glance to the blackboard that displayed 'Clay Night.'

"So, all of them have to know how to spin the wheel?" he inquired in a serious tone.

"I don't think so. The teacher works with the each student's level. I have seen many make animal masks, bird bowls, and sculptures with their hands while some are on the wheel."

"Again, I am fortunate to have flexible instructors," he said after a pause while shrugging his shoulders.

"Glad to know you are counting your blessings, man," Ronald exclaimed. "I might just drop by on the karaoke night some Saturday evening."

"Ya, right, man! See you then. I promise you will be left speechless."

That statement made Ronald ponder. "Uhh, I hope you meant speechless in a good way," he inquired with a wrinkle on his forehead and a smirk.

"Ha-ha! It could be both ways." Jay grinned. They did a fist bump and parted. As soon as he exited, a couple of loud teens entered.

"Hey, guys," Jay greeted. "The usual?"

"Yup," they both shouted in unison.

Yogi barked with joy as he approached them and sniffed their shoes. The two girls squealed and stroked his ears lovingly.

"I will also have a vegetarian bake to go with my tea, please," requested Alice, the high schooler.

"The puff or the samosa?" Jay inquired.

"Umm, I'll have the samosa this time," she said while exhibiting her purple braces. The teens were taking selfies with Yogi, all the while texting and giggling.

"Two cardamom teas with nonfat milk and one vegetarian samosa," he announced as he placed them on his counter and clinked his cash register.

As he waited for the girls to pay him, he inquired, quickly glancing at their phone screens, "Snapchatting?"

"Uh-huh! Pictures with Yogi always give us maximum views," Alice squealed as her fingers continued to tap on her screen.

"That's interesting."

"Maybe I should trademark my pet so that I can earn royalties from the clicks," he said in a serious tone calculating the amount given to him.

There was silence. Alice paused from her text and stared at him for a while before nodding in compliance. "Not a bad idea. You are a good businessman." She had a strange twinkle in her eyes that made Jay uncomfortable at first, but after a few stretches with his neck, he diverted his attention toward another group of teens entering the store.

In business for three years, he could remember regular customers who had their 'usuals' to sip. No doubt, it kept him on his toes, and he was quick with their orders too. Thus, the clinking of the cash register was heard most of the time along with the woof of Yogi who would be showered with hugs and kisses.

# CHAPTER THREE

*"Sometimes the questions are complicated and the answers are simple."* — **Dr. Seuss**

"Excuse me." A squeal was heard from the counter.

"Just a minute," Jay spoke from a distance. He was in a squatting position a few steps away from the cash register trying to clean some random spots on the floor.

"Excuse me... ee... e." The request was repeated with a higher intensity of a shriek making Yogi break from the crowd and approach the voice with quick steps.

"Be right there!" Jay pulled himself up from the floor and noticed Yogi's empty bed while walking toward the cash register looking for the person with the voice with the repeated request. There were a handful of people near the counter, some on their phone, some looking at the menu hanging on the wall, but all were waiting for him. Nevertheless, he was looking for the person with this high-pitched 'Excuse me'which had irritated him since he had to hurry to get to the counter. Now, no one owned up. He could not resist asking, "Who was it with the repeated 'Excuse me?'" he inquired in an irritating tone.

The crowd looked up at him, and then their heads went down. He followed their pattern, and his eyes went wide as his jaw dropped. "*You?*" he screeched. Everything came to a standstill. The eyes that were on their phones had moved toward these two bodies. People who were sipping their beverages either froze with their cups in their hand or placed them on the table. Conversations came to a halt as all were curious.

Adorned with soft features and a chubby figure, a girl in her mid-twenties looked up. Dressed in a sky-blue dress that touched her knees, she had a light to brown complexion with short brown-black hair. Sitting in a squatting position, she was petting Yogi. Responding to Jay's inquiry, she got up. With a height of less than four feet, she put her two hands on her hips to display her irritation. Giving out a loud sigh, she arched her eyebrows and glared back at Jay.

"Yes, it's me," she snapped with thin lips.

Jay was quick to come from behind the counter while continuing to look at her. Both continued to glare at each other rendering the people in the store invisible. When they stood facing each other, they continued with their dirty looks, their arched eyebrows, and screwed-up lips biting their tongue as if avoiding showering the other with foul language. Just then, a voice hollered from a distance that broke the trance.

"Hey! Gina Mehra, you are back!" the owner of the voice seemed to be walking toward them with brisk steps. "Long time."

Jay softened upon hearing that as he realized his loyal customer of three years was coming toward them.

He forced a smile and put his hands in his apron pocket, trying to look for something as his fingers kept fidgeting within.

"Hey!" Gina turned toward that voice with a heartwarming smile on her face. "Do I know you?" she asked in a playful voice with a frown that imbalanced her soft features and sandy complexion.

"How could you forget me?" came the young man just over five feet tall making a sulky face at her. "I'm Samuel. I used to help you set up the chairs before locking up the store every evening."

Gina gave special attention to his traits while continuing to stare at him. "You have put on weight?" She pushed her hair behind her ear that had three piercings.

Sam blushed and wanted to have more of a conversation, but Jay interrupted. "How have you been, cousin?" he asked with curiosity and a tapered tone.

"Not bad."

"How about yourself?" she inquired, scanning him from top to bottom.

Instead of replying to her question, Jay chose to ignore it and asked in a taunting way, "Why are you here?" But before she could explain, he realized the silence in his tea shop. Feeling awkward for a nanosecond, he quickly pulled her shoulder and made her stand next to him while making an announcement, "Hello, everybody, meet my cousin, Gina, from Madagascar."

At that announcement, she was quick to turn forty-five degrees and gave her typical stare. "Jamaica, not Madagascar, you idiot!"

"Ahem. Well, both are islands. So, I wouldn't care," he clarified, looking embarrassed and continued looking at his customers with a forceful smile.

"Hey! Let me take a picture of you two, just for keeps!" Samuel barged in, again.

"Seriously?" said the two cousins with a snort.

Gina paused for a bit, then she stood next to Jay for a click by Sam with a forced smile.

"So where should I send this picture?" Samuel inquired innocently.

Gina and Jay said in unison, "You have our number, Sam."

Sam, after eyeing Gina for some time, disappeared into the crowd. Mornings were usually a busy time for Got T since people wanted to fill their system with caffeine and get going with the daily humdrum.

Gina followed Jay to the back to respond to his earlier question. "It's because of you that I have traveled all these miles," she revealed.

"Huh?" Jay stopped and turned one hundred eighty degrees to face her.

"Yes."

He snorted to which she grunted in return. Then after a few breaths, she confessed, "I have finished all my coursework and am now working on my thesis for my Masters in Psychology. So, I thought who better a candidate than my cousin."

Jay became more irritated. "And you think I will not only be your object of study, but I will also open my home to you?"

"Not at all." She was frank and stern. Raising her hands in the air, she added, "I will be your assistant in this store as I did two years ago and also pay you for lodging and eating."

"I will not let you off so easy, cousin. How about some compensation for being your object of study, too?" He beamed, grabbing some cups from the top shelf. Crossing her eyebrows, she bit her lip and kept tapping her left foot as if in deep thought. Her object of study was standing patiently half expecting a million-dollar deal in return.

"Done!" she declared with her right arm in the air.

That made him arch his eyebrows. "Done what?" he asked irritatingly. Just then, a bell rang from across the cash register breaking their conversation.

"Hold that thought," he blurted. "Customers are next to God," he declared and dashed toward the counter. She giggled with raised eyebrows and followed him like a gnome.

Once Jay took the order, she was quick to start fulfilling it. "Are you sure?" he inquired in an earnest tone.

"Sure about what?" she paused to ask.

"That you want to start working today?" There was a pause, and he continued, "I mean you can take it easy today if you want. Start fresh tomorrow."

"No, I'm good," she said as she was mixing the contents. That impressed him.

"You have not forgotten a thing?" he observed.

"What's to forget? Making tea can be any dimwit's job," she commented without any remorse. "Besides, your menu is the same as the last time I visited you two years ago." She shrugged in her defense. He squinted. She gave an evil smile in return.

"Sure, any dimwit's job. But to make profits from it, that's what makes that person clever and adept," he spoke his justification.

She scrunched her nose for a bit. "I actually agree with you. Not everyone knows how to make cash out of every situation. I like that blackboard displaying the plan for each weeknight," she admitted, wiping the cup clean before calling out the number indicating the order is ready.

Jay was struck at first, but he had hidden the trait of being presumptuous and arrogant under his mattress each morning when he would step out for work. People he loved had taken it in his stride. "Yes, I agree," he said shamelessly, "So, tell me what will I gain from being your object of study?"

"What is the going rate of hourly pay?" she inquired.

"Thirteen dollars and fifty cents."

"Pay me ten dollars. Plus, I will pay for my boarding and lodging unlike my last visit."

"Your last visit was a recreational one courtesy of your summer break from your Master's program," Jay clarified.

"Yes, indeed. So, does that sound like a deal?" She extended her hand toward him. He scratched his head at first trying to decipher if anything looked fishy, but then after a few seconds' pause, their hands met.

"Cousin, you want to sign some papers?" she inquired, knowing his true temperament.

"Nah! I trust you, G," he said in a blatant tone and went about his chores.

**********

Samuel could not contain himself. His golden heart refused to catch the cold vibes that Gina threw at him. The news of Gina coming back went viral within a few hours. As instructed by her new boss, she was in the storage room sorting things and finding her companion who was buried deep somewhere in there. She was in awe as to how the store's business had picked up since she last visited Jay. The number of disposable cups, napkins, plates, and silverware said it all. "Aha! There you are!" She picked up the stepping stool and dusted it well, knowing this would be her constant mate when she'd need to reach out over the high counters and shelves.

Amidst all this was Mike, the dog walker for Yogi. He knocked on the window facing the register in a peculiar fashion, and that was enough to make the adrenaline rush in Yogi. He jumped off his dog bed and began to bounce around frantically in excitement, forcing Jay to forget everything, even his current customer. He quickly leashed his pet and handed the rein to the dog walker who was holding the straps of many breeds including Brussels griffon, English toy spaniel, Chinese crested, Japanese chin, Maltese, pug, and Pomeranian.

"I always wonder how you can handle all eight dogs in one go," would be Jay's favorite dialogue which he would always mutter in appreciation. One of Mike's favored responses was, "I wouldn't mind taking twenty in a go. Alas, I have only ten fingers, so I shall keep it limited for now."

While in the café, Gina met many visitors who had warm memories of her when she had visited Jay's store two years ago. The fervor was infectious, and she did not mind responding to the same questions over and over again. Jay was also enjoying the visitors since he would not lose any opportunity to click that register and get more orders.

Once the crowd had subsided, Gina could not resist. "I love what you have done to this place. You are expanding, and I am impressed by all these weeknight events you have planned. How do you do it?" she asked enthusiastically with her hands on her hips and blowing her bangs off her forehead.

Jay paused from his cleaning and asked, "How do I do what?"

"Keep your old customers? I'm seeing them after two years, but it seems they are stuck here in time."

He chortled. "Many reasons... many reasons contribute to it."

He made himself comfortable on the barstool to explain with pride, "First and foremost, I have maintained the quality of my products. Second, I'm the boss as well as the employee giving each of my customers all my attention. Third, is my memory. I make it a point to remember them when they visit the next time, giving them the spotlight. Fourth, and very important, I have tried to keep my prices to the bare minimum."

"You make it sound so simple," Gina complimented him.

He was quick to accept it. "Man is a social animal, Gina. That's the foremost thing I learned the first day of my MBA class." He smiled and started working on his baking for the evening event.

"Do you make any profits, then?" she asked genuinely. "Because the spices don't come cheap."

"I have wholesale vendors, and that allows me to save quite a bit. With regards to profits, yes, I'm about to scratch off the biggest item off my wish list," he said with glee as his lips stretched from one ear to the other with his eyes widening with joy that was both authentic and sincere.

"Are you serious? So, you are following the agenda of your therapist. Wow, I am impressed." She sounded very excited about it but then raised her eyebrows. "Wait. Don't tell me. Ahem. Let me guess..." She scrunched her nose, wrinkled her eyebrows, trying to remember the conversation they had two years ago where each of them had talked about their dreams and goals.

She remembered this conversation very vividly since havoc was created in his house over her mere suggestion. Plates with contents of food were smashed on the floor as he pulled the tablecloth in anger. The dining chair was flung down, and his blaring tone made it very clear that she should never cross that line of his past. Jay, on the other hand, had forgotten that incident. Maybe since the struggle to stay in the present for him was appalling that he forgot when someone tried to shake hands with him over his past. He was thrilled that she was trying to remember.

"Beach house?" she inquired with her index finger up.

He nodded with arched eyebrows and a satisfied smile as if a toddler is on the right path to recitation.

"Tesla?" she raised her middle finger.

"Uh-huh!" he nodded with patience and a slight smile.

"Cruising in the Pacific?" she raised her ring finger.

"Bang on!" He went and high-fived her. "Drinks and lunch will always be on the house for you!"

She sneered at his comment. "You're such a typical businessman."

"What?"

She just waved to let go of this topic.

While she was busy cutting and chopping the ingredients, she asked casually, "So, been in touch with Sasha?" There was silence. Her back was facing him, and she could feel the glare on her back. She slowly turned to face him. "I'm sorry, I didn't realize it's still a raw bruise."

He snickered, getting back to doing his stuff while admitting that the wound had not healed. He tried to keep his emotions in check amidst the disclosure. She did not hesitate to wrap her short arms around his waist. That was the highest she could reach.

"Damn this height," she muttered.

He paused for a bit to take in her embrace, and then they split apart. Baring emotions were neither cousin's favorite thing to do. They loved showering each other with swearing to show their affection, making this a very weird moment for both of them. They muttered something while brushing either their hair or clothes as if to get the other's energy off them before getting back to work. The awkwardness was busted since customers and their orders kept pouring in.

**********

The clock was ticking, and the brightest star was nearing the horizon tainting the sky with orange and yellow hues. Jay noticed the change in the surroundings and was quick to remark, "G, nature beckons you."

Gina didn't waste a minute. She was quick to take this opportunity, hung her apron and grabbed something in her fist from her purse she kept in the storage room. She stepped out and was in awe of the painting the universe had created. The clouds were like cotton candy blushing at the warm touch of the sun. A flock of sparrows flew home across the magenta sky. Her eyes were steady toward the horizon with the last orange rays making her face glow. Her lips gave a slightly twitched smile indicating the kind of memories she had transported herself to.

That picture reminded her of so many memories. Her childhood evenings spent with her dad in their small apartment balcony, which was a mere two feet by two feet. But the fun and the laughter they shared skipping rope and rolling the ball was still heard. The many trips she made with her parents to places such as the Robber's Cave, the Rajaji's National Park, the Timber Museum, the Sahasradhara Waterfalls in their ambassador car were all endearing, not to mention the many times their car needed a jump-start even though it was considered the 'King of Indian Roads.' She beamed when she recollected how her mom fought with her friends for teasing her.

When her stunted growth was diagnosed, her parents' support was incredible. They had formed a barrier around her and kept her shielded. She also envisioned her parents along with Jay's as they would sit on his big luscious lawn to have tea on various occasions while these two would jump, hop, and skip around. A smile soon faded as she also remembered the day when Jay's mom gave her the news about her parents' demise. She distinctly remembered that as she was combing her doll's golden hair. The doll was her last gift from her parents, and she still has that figurine tucked away in one of the bags in her apartment in Jamaica.

A tear fell on her cheek, and it brought her out of her reverie. The sunset then and the sunset today have not changed. Time is still constant for her, except the people around her have been replaced.

The cool air gave her goosebumps, and she was quick to wipe them away embracing herself with her short arms realizing the dip in the temperature. After a couple of breaths, she opened her fist, and soon she was rolling small puffs with her cigarette. At first, they were quick, wanting to get the whiff of tobacco into her system, and then the speed reduced as she breathed in deep and exhaled at her leisure.

She tapped her feet as if still trying to come to terms with the loss of her parents, and periodically smiled to a passerby.

*Those gentle words of Usha aunty were still ringing in her ears. She hugged her from the side while conveying the news, "Gina, I have some news for you. Your parents' car was in a crash, and they are hurt."*

*"How much hurt?" asked eleven-year-old Gina with wide eyes*

*"Very badly hurt," she spoke with a choke in her throat.*

*Seeing the perplexed look in Gina's eyes, she continued, "Gina, your parents are no more." With that, the aunt hugged the pre-teen.*

*Gina felt no emotion. She stayed in her embrace and noticed the sunset from her arms, refusing to let go. Little did she realize that this sunset would be her best friend from then on. Just then, ten-year-old Jay entered the scene and was jealous seeing her in his mom's embrace. Usha quickly grabbed him with her other arm and embraced both the children with silent sobs.*

*Life changed in a whirlwind as Usha and Anil adopted Gina. Living with her maternal grandparents, adopted parents, and Jay was quite a change with frequent episodes of sobbing and nightmares, but gradually love overtook, and she settled in. Needless to say, memories never faded until she made a point to say hello and goodbye to sunsets in any part of the world.*

********

Jay was setting down the platter with the baked goods and wiping the cash counter before the evening's event when his eyes fell on the clock, and he heard a familiar tap on his big, wide side window. The blinds were partially down to avoid the sun's rays from penetrating and disturbing the customers, so no one paid heed to the knock except Jay. He was quick to pour ingredients into a cup along with a couple of eats in a brown bag and rushed to the entrance. Yogi woofed, and his master acknowledged it with a 'sit' command and proceeded. At that moment, he thanked the service dog agency that had him trained.

Jay walked past Gina ignoring her presence and went toward the side of his store where the knock came from to hand the cup and brown bag to a lady. Her gloved hands took them, and she bowed to show her gratitude. Jay reciprocated with a bow. There was silence, but a lot was being communicated with these gestures. Gina was observing all this from a distance. She was shocked and astonished beyond words. Her cousin was giving something to someone without accepting cash! She was aware that after the turmoil he had been through, he did not trust any relationship, and the concept of money trading hands always made him comfortable and not cheated.

With that in mind, she felt something fishy and could not contain herself. She was quick to throw the butt of her cigarette on the floor, stomp on it to extinguish the hot ashes, and walked toward them with quick steps before they could part in different directions.

"Hey!" She tried to get their attention. The lady was covered with different color drapes around her, including her face, keeping only her eyes and mouth bare. There was a microsecond of eye contact between Gina and the woman before she opened her umbrella and started walking slowly away, all the while holding the crooked handle and maneuvering the umbrella's end facing Gina. At that moment, Jay turned toward the voice and raised his hand trying to stop Gina, but she was on a mission. She ran past him while pushing his hand away and tried to shoo the umbrella past the lady's face. She was not only determined to know who this lady was, but now she was also intrigued by this lady's choice of clothing.

*Why the heck is she covered all over with clothes?*

Gina managed to get a peek into her eyes, and they spoke so many emotions. There was fear followed by kindness and compassion in them. That confused her, her pace slowed, and as a result, she lost sight of her. Jay caught up to her and held her shoulder. "Please! Don't create a scene here," he urged.

His cousin was quick to turn around. "About what? You are the one who is displaying a dramatic performance." Her eyes glared at him, and he did not have the courage to argue but just came to the point.

"I will let you in on it once we are home."

She frowned, and he nodded with a couple of blinks as if trying to pacify her. As they were headed back to his store, he twitched his nose and questioned with authority, "What the heck, Gina. Since when?"

"Huh?"

"Your breath says it all." He frowned.

Gina was quick to turn her face in the other direction and licked her wrist. Jay could not refrain. "Now you are behaving like Yogi. What's got into you?" He snickered. She glared back at him, and then smelled that spot on her wrist where she left her mark. That smell made her frown.

Jay asked with authority, "What is this?"

"Huh! What is what?" his cousin asked with a sneer. He was quick to bring her arm around and point out the butt on the floor. She shrugged her shoulders and tried to play defensive. "So, I smoke when I need to calm my nerves."

"Why do you need to calm your nerves?"

"Goddammit, I have traveled seven hours to be here. My mind and body ache," she yelped.

"Well, who asked you to start working today?" There was a pause.

"Who said I was working for you. I needed to start working on my research starting today, so I did not want to go home and rest." Gina clarified. "Oh! Come on! Quit this!" he said with a plea.

"Have you quit your old habits?" she arched her eyebrows and questioned him.

He shrugged his shoulders. "Okay, chill, cousin. It's your life. You choose to destroy yourself..." He raised his hands in the air and took Yogi in another direction to lighten his bladder. She just rolled her eyes and continued to stare at the colors in the sky.

# CHAPTER FOUR

*"You've got to find yourself first. Everything else'll follow."* —
**Charles de Lint**


The clock struck seven, and Jay made sure the thermostat exhibited seventy degrees Fahrenheit to keep his customers warm while they were there. The air outside was brisk and cool, perfect weather to grab a hot beverage and read. Young adults started pouring in. The aroma was alluring with the fresh batch of baked goods in the oven. Each of them had a book or a tablet in their hand. After finding space for themselves, they got in line to order their food.

"Gina, could you please pop in a mint?" he asked. "I don't want you to have a foul smell while serving my customers." At first, Gina was taken back.

She arched her eyebrows, and after a couple of breaths, she spoke. "Smarty pants! Do you think you are the only hygienic person around here?" She kept staring at him. "I have done what is needed."

Jay whispered, "Thank you" with a gracious smile, but she did not look amused.

Jay made it a point to talk to each customer before taking their respective orders. Simultaneously, he also introduced his cousin, Gina, to each of them. Gina could detect the warmth in his voice and was very curious as to how his transformation came about. She arched her eyebrows for a second at this new side to him.

As she was preparing the orders, "Hello," "Nice to meet you," and "How have you been?" were the standard pleasantries she exchanged between the avid book readers. Soon the book club was in session.

"So, what's the book about? Did you read it, Jay?" she whispered to him. "Do you have the book?"

"*Two by Two* by Nicholas Sparks, and yes and yes," he muttered before calling out the customer's name for her order.

"Jeez! You are too professional."

"Busy time." He winked at her. Soon the moderator of the book club arrived.

"Darlene, how have you been?" Jay gave her a warm welcome. Pausing at the entrance to get a visual, she waved to everyone while checking out the deli. The concoction of the delicious aromas hanging in the air from the baked food and the different spices brewing in the kitchen along with the new girl behind the counter with Jay drew her in toward Jay and Gina.

Each reader discussed *Two by Two* at length. The quotes from the book were flying everywhere. Jay caught a particular one, and fancied it by muttering under his breath, *"Do you remember what I said about friendship? It's about someone who walks into your life, says I'm here for you and then proves it."*

Gina was cautious about where this could lead. She tried to ignore him while seating herself next to one of the reviewers and keeping a keen ear on the discussions in the room.

"Russ is not an ideal person. I felt irritated at his stupidity of not taking a stand against his wife, Vivian, in the first place," said one reviewer while the others nodded in agreement. "Vivian, on the other hand, is a terrible person."

"Jeez, the characters are not likable by the readers, so how did they continue reading this book?" speculated Gina chewing on a bite of samosa.

"But the book centers on the complications that arise in a relationship at any time. It talks about how we overlook the problematic characteristics of a person just because we are madly in love with them. It explores the transformations a person can go through to cope up with these situations," said another reviewer in the room.

Gina's eyes widened as if he had read her mind, but it also made her cautious after hearing what was said. She tried to look for Jay, hoping he wasn't listening to these comments since relationships are a sensitive topic for him. She was worried he could explode. Fortunately, he was nowhere in sight.

"But you know what I especially enjoyed reading was the relationship of the father and child. The bond they shared was magical, beautiful, and realistic," said a bespectacled reviewer with dimples in between sipping her ginger tea. "I feel Nicholas Sparks is the king when it comes to emotions and love," she added with dreamy eyes.

Heads nodded. Gina was quick to eye Jay and was relieved to see him with his headphones on. He was busy scrubbing the counter. Although the next second, she frowned wondering if he always did this, but then she relaxed. *It's for the better or else I would have a tough night since I am bunking at his place. Phew.*

Blinking a couple of times, she came to terms with her thoughts and went back to listening to the readers' views and thoughts.

"Have you read the book?" Nudged a reader to Gina. She was quick to nod her head negatively.

"I do not wish to spoil *Two by Two* for you, but then I would definitely love to know your views after you're done reading it." Gina glanced sideways and appreciated his concern with a gentle nod wanting to go back to listening to the others' views, but this guy continued, "You know..." he slurped his iced tea in between, "... as the book progresses, there is an unexpected twist in the tale, and I just loved it," he said with a wide smile that showed off his uneven teeth.

"Good for you!" Gina cut through and redirected her eyes toward the table where people were having a serious discussion. She loved the conversations in spite of her not having read the book. Maybe since family, love, and friendship were the virtues she so dearly loved, but life had never given her an opportunity to embrace them, just as if a person wants to ride in an E-Class Mercedes but never got an opportunity to do so, neither is there sorrow or joys, just a sheer craving for it.

"More emphasis has been made on the family and how people who love us are always there to help with any hurdle in life. The book talks about recovery, lost love, and friendship," Darlene concluded as they were nearing the end of the night's event while asking for suggestions for another title for next week. The club voted for a book entitled *Map of the Heart* by Susan Wiggs, and the meeting ended.

Gina loved what she heard, and while promising her table neighbor to read it and let him know her views at the next meeting, she was thankful her cousin was present but not present in this discussion.

# CHAPTER FIVE

*"It is one thing to lose people you love. It is another to lose yourself. That is a greater loss."*
— **Donna Goddard**

"Remind me to wear a jacket," complained Gina loudly, striding toward her car when her eyes fell on Jay's car. "Jeez, upgrade?"

"Yes, I know. I'm getting there. My bucket list will soon allow me to drive home in a Tesla." He grinned. She clicked on her remote to open the door of her Ford Focus SUV rental.

"Wow! Nice. You never think of being frugal, huh?" he mocked at her choice.

"Why should I?" she defended. "My parents left me a fortune. I have nobody to leave my fortune to. Why shouldn't I enjoy it?" she questioned in an earnest tone. "Besides considering my height, a SUV works for me," she justified, then inquired, "In fact, your mom and our grandparents keep nudging you, too. Why don't you?"

He got uncomfortable discussing the topic. "Will see you at home. I might be late. Here's the key. You know your way around my place so make yourself comfortable." He smiled beckoning Yogi to climb into the passenger seat.

Gina had a frown at first, but then without questioning, she took the key before confirming the address, and the cousins went their way. She entered the address in her GPS and was looking forward to the feeling of home after a long flight. Even though the surroundings were dark, she kept having *déjà-vu* moments every time she crossed landmarks such as the often-visited ice cream store, the Velcro Mall whose name she still found funny and remembered getting hooked to it on her first visit, frequenting it until the day she boarded her to Madagascar.

The stores in this mall were unique as were their products. Even a particular crossing made her travel into the past to a time when she had jumped the signal and was stopped by a cop. The face of the cop and their conversation was fresh in her mind, making her blush and grin at the same time. Her thoughts were interrupted when a soft voice announced, "Your destination is on the left. You have arrived."

Taking a left turn, she giggled. *Time flies when you walk old paths. Also, it's therapeutic to drive here versus the erratic driving in Jamaica.*

Gina unlocked the main door and immediately found herself engulfed in memories that still lingered long after she had left this town two years ago. The decor was as is, making her cringe at first, but then she took it in stride while walking past the living room and dining area. She glanced quickly into the kitchen. Nothing had changed, not even the paintings on the wall.

The cream-color couch had black marks on it, and the dining table had scratches around its legs. The new addition was the dog bowls and a few toys that lay scattered around. No doubt Yogi was to be blamed for the mess. *Hmm... Americans are known to change their things every two years. He is where I left him.* She gave a quick peek into her cousin's bedroom hoping to find a picture frame of a girl, but all seemed constant and boring.

She yawned and went to the other room, which had meager accessories. The neat and organized twin-size bed made her feel at ease enough to push her to freshen up in the attached bathroom and change into her pajamas. Lazing on the bed, she checked her messages for a bit and then headed to the kitchen. Just as she opened the refrigerator, the ringing of the doorbell startled her. She did not have to second-guess since she could hear the woof of Yogi after that.

The aroma whiffed through the seams of the door hinges. "Aha, food."

Then she complained, "Why didn't you tell me where you were going? We could have managed?"

"I thought since it's your first day here, I ought to serve you something decent."

"Serve me?" She widened her eyes. "I thought I was supposed to pay for my boarding and lodging?"

He mocked at her statement. "G, you have not changed a bit. You tend to inscribe every statement of mine in gold," he said irritatingly.

"I don't want to be a burden on you," she declared with shrugged shoulders, sitting cross-legged on the dining chair while observing the cabinets that he opened to get the cutlery and dinnerware.

"You are not, and never will be. In fact, I'm always delighted when you visit me," he said with a gleam in his eyes that was worth a million dollars. She was touched by it but could not handle it either.

"Since when did you start speaking from your heart?"

That unexpected affront irritated him. "Okay, cut it. You can plan your expenses starting tomorrow. Fill up the pantry according to your likings, and remember you ought to clean up after you eat, sleep, and even shit," he said in a mordant tone.

"Jay! Nooo... not when we are about to eat. Dammit!" Gina was equally forthright.

"You wanted policies, so I handed them to you," he commanded, pouring water in the dog bowl for Yogi.

She admired the scene. "Yogi is even more adorable than the picture you sent me when you adopted him."

Jay beamed with pride.

She ignored him and dug into the bowls to serve some Pad Thai, coconut rice, ginger-garlic tofu, and red chicken curry on her plate.

"Food is yummy. Is that from the same Krung Thai restaurant?"

"Aha!"

"Aww, you know me so well."

Without responding, he simply served food on his plate and sat facing her. Yogi was going back and forth with the hope that someone would drop a speck of food.

"You are done with dinner, Yogi," Jay said in a punitive tone only to find the beagle staring at him with puppy eyes.

"Aww... let's give him some food," pleaded Gina.

"No, I don't serve him human food."

"What? But we always used to feed our dogs in India. What's so special about these dogs here?" inquired Gina putting a spoonful of rice in her mouth.

In a bid to change the topic, Jay began his inquiry. Sounding very much like an elder sibling who is inquisitive about his little sister, he said, "So tell me, what are your plans after you finish your thesis? Do you plan on finding a job there, or do you want to immigrate to another country?"

"It depends on where I get a job. Will your country give me one?" she asked with a cackle.

Jay chortled over it. "So, you can come visit me more often?"

"Why not? We are family, and we have practically grown up together as siblings." She eyed him carefully and spoke with caution, "I really wonder what made you drift away."

His brain once again signaled an alert as the topic was drifting toward things he didn't want to discuss. He again tried changing the subject. "So, are you seeing anybody out there?"

This time she refused to respond and continued eating, jabbing her piece of chicken into the curry. There was silence because even Yogi was bored and showed his displeasure at not getting any crumbs to nibble on by sitting in one corner. They both finished their food and pitched in to clean the kitchen spotless.

"I usually start to work early. But you can come in around nine in the morning," he suggested and pulled out his sales sheet to calculate his profits for the day.

She nodded in compliance and went to her room. After a few minutes, there was a knock on her door. Jay walked in with some bed sheets and a towel. She thanked him curtly and went back to writing notes in her diary. He was curious. "Is that about me?"

Gina peeked through her glasses and glanced at him. "Yes," she responded in a crude manner.

"Could I see your analysis?"

"Nope," she replied, again with a very blunt response. "I'm under no obligation to show you my research. This is the reason I have offered to pay you for being my object of study."

Jay nodded his head while arching his eyebrows and turned to head out of the room, shutting the door after him.

She felt lousy and tried deep breathing with closed eyes to calm down.

*History with ego was playing a major role in both their lives. These two souls had grown up together and had seen adversities but refused to pour their heart out, which was creating cracks in their relationship. Unfortunately, time was ticking.*

# CHAPTER SIX

*"Sometimes that which you have never lost is the hardest to find."* — **Iva Kenaz**

The night went by peacefully as no nightmares haunted Jay. However, both he and Yogi woke up at the crack of dawn going about their usual business. Jay heard Gina's door crack open when he was brewing his cup of coffee.

"'Morning." She greeted him with a smile.

Yogi was quick to come and greet her followed by a cheery greeting from Jay. "Coffee?"

"Yes, please. Would you happen to have half-and-half?" she inquired.

"Nah, just one percent." He poured another cup for her.

"No worries. I plan to go grocery shopping later this morning and stock up on my supplies," she said with confidence while grabbing the cup from him that looked chalky because of the milk and helped herself to some cookies.

"How was your night? Sleep well?" He tried sounding concerned.

"Aha!" She took a few sips from her cup and immediately made a disgusted face while shaking her head twice. Jay chuckled.

"I need to get my groceries today for sure. I need my supplies to stay alert and focused so that I can finish my research and get out of here," she said matter of factly.

"About that..." He cleared his throat and drew up a chair next to her. She eyed him carefully since she had never seen him so serious.

"You know I have items on my bucket list."

She nodded, biting into a biscuit and immediately scowled, "Eww... who has almond butter cookies in the morning? Yuck."

She tried hard not to choke and keep her focus on him.

"So, I have enough funds to buy a car for myself."

"Wow! Let's go car shopping then." She raised her hands excitedly, momentarily forgetting the horrible coffee and cookies.

"No... no! Stop that thought." He moved his head from right to left.

"What now?" She became confused.

"Instead, I was thinking since you are here, I might as well go for a week- long cruise in the Pacific."

Surprised at this suggestion, she paused to find the right words but couldn't, so she just burst out, "You are such an opportunist, Jay."

Fuming with anger, she continued, "Have you forgotten? I have come here to do my research, and the object of study is you. Just you. Do you not get it?" She was trying to keep her voice in check as Yogi was going about in circles sensing her anger.

Jay, on the other hand, was patient. "Yes, Gina, I understand the reason you are visiting me. But, I have it all planned out," he said with a brief smile trying to put down the logistics before her, but she just got up and walked to his backyard with Yogi tagging along.

Jay looked at his watch and muttered, "Damn," and followed her.

She was admiring the little vegetation he had in his garden. The camellias, the gerbera daisies, and the carnations were blooming, however, the shrubs were uneven and needed attention along with the small patch of grass which needed mowing. "Hmm... interesting yard you have here," she complimented him. "Are you the caretaker?"

"Well yes and no," he confessed, scratching his head in between sipping his coffee.

After a brief pause, he said, "Yogi also plays an important role by adding manure to it." He cackled over his comment. The name was enough for a woof from his beagle, and Gina was quick to pet him.

Jay was quick to come back to his conversation. "Now coming back to our previous discussion, I will give one full week to being your object of research. While you were making notes, I, too, was busy reading about the kind of work a person needs to do to research." He paused. "The analyst also needs to study the surroundings of the object of the research. So, while I will be away, you can question the people with whom I interact with daily to reach your conclusion."

He waited for a response, but since Gina was contemplating it while rubbing Yogi's fur, he jumped in. "You see it's a win-win situation for both of us. While I tick off one of my items off my bucket list, you can finish off your research without any interruption." He extended his hands wide as if trying to show her the plan is so simple. "You see, I wouldn't have any better person to take care of my store in my absence than you." Then he tilted his head to look at her with puppy eyes.

"All right, all right. I will do it," she announced dramatically while getting up and starting to walk inside.

"Yes," Jay exclaimed with joy, and Yogi woofed at him while wagging his tail energetically.

"Atta boy!" Leading his pet inside, he patted his ears in a playful manner while cleaning the little mess left behind by Yogi after his breakfast in the kitchen. Before leaving, Jay tapped on Gina's bedroom door to notify her about the spare key to the home. Once she acknowledged, the duo left for work as he grabbed his jacket to protect him from the low temperature of the November mornings.

# CHAPTER SEVEN

*"You must befriend a few skeletons before you'll find your
deepest self."*
**— Curtis Tyrone Jones**

Gina took a leisurely bath dressing casually in a pair of
jeans and plaid shirt. She adorned herself with dangling
earrings and bracelets, dabbing her medium skin tone with
a moisturizing lotion before heading out for grocery store.

Save-Way Mart was just a block away, so the drive was
quick, and soon she was pushing her shopping cart into the
store. The wide aisles displayed arrays of fresh produce,
fruits, vegetables, and flowers. The vibrant colors brought a
smile to her lips. She enjoyed picking up her favorite fruits
and placing them in her cart.

She loved what she saw especially since Kingston City
did not offer all these luxuries. As she walked leisurely
through the aisles, she recollected how she was adamant
about studying in Jamaica's capital for her Master's despite
the constant negativity from her maternal grandparents
and Jay's mom. She had received three white envelopes
with 'Accepted' from Chicago University, NYU, and the
Tufts, but she wanted a tropical climate and an out-of-box
experience.

Life changed for her. She learned to cook, care for
herself, and even learned to lick her bruises although Usha

aunty was just a text away, but she wanted to grow up and took pride in her decision. Her thoughts exhibited through her body language.

She was walking straight, chin up with a confident smile while moving through the aisles and picking out food that delighted her senses. She did not hesitate to put anything to her liking in the cart. When the cash register clicked the numbers, she realized she had shopped for almost a month's supply while placing her items in the brown grocery bags. At first, she was apprehensive and thought of returning some stuff but then realized the deal Jay had proposed. Loneliness and boredom always made her eat more, so she was confident that this entire ration would be consumed while he was away on his holiday.

She smiled while unloading the brown bags into his kitchen realizing the space constraint she was going to face. She tried finding space for the many cereal boxes, the various kinds of biscuits, and boxes of granola bars in his cupboards while stepping on the dining chair to put them away, courtesy her short height.

At first, she cursed her physical stature but immediately corrected her thoughts,

*Thank God it's just my height that got truncated due to some defect in my gene pool. Life would have been miserable if I had some other physical defect, especially with no parents around to sheath me from this wild world.*

She dumped the boxes of frozen entrees into the freezer while placing fresh fruits such as apples, bananas, mangoes, and grapes on the kitchen counter. Fresh vegetables, milk, eggs, bread, and condiments such as ketchup and syrup were placed in the almost-empty refrigerator.

While devouring a heavy breakfast comprised of pancakes, eggs, and toast, she flipped through the various channels on the television. She felt as if she were in a five-star hotel and did not mind doing the cooking and cleaning thereafter. Soon, she headed out carrying her purse and a fleece jacket.

Thanks to the daylight, the drive to the store was even more significant not allowing her to go beyond fifteen miles per hour, but at the same time, it gave her ample opportunity to assess her surroundings. The traffic was heavy causing her to stop at every stoplight. The greenery around had faded thanks to the drought California was facing. The number of stores had increased, and so did the total number of cars on the road. "Economy is doing well," she muttered all the while following the directions courtesy of the GPS.

"Good morning," came a cheery and audible greeting from the owner of Got T as she stepped into the store. Yogi was quick to greet her with a big jump that reached her bosom. She was quick to reciprocate by a gentle and fond rub on his ears. She did not hesitate to comment on his chirpy greeting.

"I always greet everyone who enters my store."

She cut in, "Sure, because they are your customers. What will you get from me?" After a brief pause, she winked. "And now I, too, would be loved since I agreed to look after your store while you go on your vacation, huh?" she said with arched eyebrows before pouring a cardamom tea for herself.

At first, Jay screwed his lips since truth is always bitter, but then he came to terms with it and just let it go.

The clinking of the cash register, the array of cups being prepared and picked up by the customers was going at a steady rate. Customers were usually brief—they would come and leave. School hours made the seating in the store to the bare minimum, leaving them all with ample time to talk while taking care of drinks.

"Did you book your cruise ticket? What's your itinerary?"

"I'm researching it. I am thinking of driving to Los Angeles and boarding the cruise from there. My idea is to go on a cruise in the Pacific," he shared with her.

"Okay, so then look it up. Although the ticket will be expensive, I guess you have a good bargain with someone attending to your store and Yogi while you're away on a holiday, huh?" she said candidly.

"Yogi?" Jay questioned in a confused tone. "No way! He is my partner and will be joining me on this cruise," he said in an affirmative tone.

"But, are dogs allowed on a cruise?" she blurted out abruptly and then tried to clarify, "I mean with so many humans, these canines could have stranger's anxiety or some sort of behavioral disorder..." and further lowering her voice, "... and that could create a ruckus on the ship." She blinked a couple of times trying to reason.

After a brief pause, Jay commented, "You are correct. That's why I had to fill out a questionnaire about my pet. There were questions such as his breed, age, weight, and his mannerisms asking if he is potty trained, and they even inquired if he barks unnecessarily," Jay said in an informative tone.

"Cool!" Gina was impressed, but still was not convinced. "So, why not take a human with you on a holiday?"

Jay got the vibes. "Look, Yogi and I decided to do this a long time ago, so I can't turn my back on him now."

She scrunched her eyebrows. "Jeez! You need to get a life. Do you have any friends beyond your customers and your dog?" she said in a cynical tone.

He did not like those words but chose to ignore her.

The store was demanding with endless clinks of the register, and thanks to Gina's help, he could take a break now and then to research the cruise. After hours of drifting, Jay found the perfect deal for a week-long holiday.

"Is tonight chess night?" Gina inquired while chopping the ingredients for more baking for the evening.

"Aha! The coordinator, Azra, gets the chess-boards and supplies. We just have to get our eats ready," he said with a wink and then continued, "You know this is such perfect timing since you were already introduced to everyone."

Jay sounded very confident as he eyed Gina, but she looked lost in thought staring out the window. The sky was orange in color, and the sun was about to set. She was quick to glance outside, the end of the day making him sigh deeply. "Gina, you never need permission to do what you always do!" She gave him a side glimpse and rushed out the front door. Sunsets and Gina are like siblings who have a love-hate relationship.

He brought his attention back to the store and started arranging the vacant tables with a pair of chairs on each side of them for the next meeting. Though occupied, subconsciously he was also staying alert for that knock on his side window.

As soon as he heard the knock, he was quick to put all the things together. The speed with which he moved to gather her order was stupendous. He could sleepwalk through it all and still get it right. While rushing out with that brown bag and a cup, his eyes fell on Gina. She didn't bother to race toward them this time but just observed from a distance.

Walking back to the store, he appreciated her patience and nodded with gratitude. "You know I will be taking care of the store next week. You ought to tell me, or I will not be serving that masked woman," she said in a derisive tone.

Jay gulped, "Give me some time. How about when I come back, I will tell you everything?" he appealed.

She squinted and then nodded in disbelief. "Seriously? What's so special about that lady? And why is she wrapped up like a mummy, for God's sake?" Waving her hands in the air, she wanted him to understand her desperation.

"Gina, please," he requested, walking back into the store.

The clock struck seven, and people started pouring in. Along came Azra with a big bag on wheels. At first, he was apologetic to the bystanders and then quickly set up the tables with the chessboards and a timer on each.

His long, crooked nose was holding the eyeglasses that helped him read the names of people interested in playing, and he had taken the liberty to pair them up. Dropping off their fees for that evening in a jute box, they would be seated opposite to the name called out.

Jay was anxious as to who he would be paired with, his anxiety clearly visible in his actions. He was constantly rubbing his hands and wiping them clean on his apron.

Gina could not resist. "You play, too?"

"Aha, I have checkmated three players." He had a wide smile with a genuine gleam in his eyes as he adjusted his shoulders. Gina noted his expression.

"Jay..." Azra uttered his name, "... you will play against Toby."

Jay came forward. He put his fees in the box and sat on one chair waiting for Toby. Azra announced the name again. No response. Azra shrugged his shoulder and was about to call out another name when a cold draft entered as the door opened.

"Sorry I'm late," a shrill voice apologized followed by squeaky laughter.

"Azra?" she questioned as her heels click-clacked toward him. Her petite figure wearing a pencil skirt and loose floral top ensured all eyes were on her.

"Hi, I'm Toby," she announced, extending her hand toward him. The teacher chose to nod instead. She hesitated all the while playing with her long blonde hair tied in a ponytail for a bit while biting her lips. She then placed her fees in the box and looked around with a meek expression on her face.

"Please sit there," Azra spoke in a serious tone while pointing toward the table. "You will be playing against Jay. I heard from your coach, who happens to be a good friend of mine, that you are good."

She nodded a couple of times blinking her big brown eyes making her golden bangs collide on her forehead, followed by high-pitched laughter.

"Jay, my student is equally good. I matched you with her based on both your timings," he said with a smile.

Jay got up to shake hands with her. He was equally pleased to meet his competitor.

"What made you come to this town?" Azra inquired while Toby occupied a seat opposite Jay.

"I changed jobs recently, and this place is close to my work so..." she said with a screech.

The people in the store would raise their eyebrows every time she would speak, while Gina giggled behind the register.

Once everyone was seated, they took a five-minute break, and the register began clicking. Drinks and eats were ordered making Jay a happy owner.

Soon everyone got back to their seat, and the game started. Gina observed, but mostly she was eyeing her object of research. Jay was observing his opponent closely. She would make her move, tap the clock, and then clench her fist and closing her eyes making a snickering laugh. He found it very amusing and wanted to keep her at ease, deliberately delaying his move by tapping the clock after a few seconds of contemplation. She would then give out a high-pitched scream.

Players in the café would be distracted while Jay, on the other hand, was quite amused and didn't seem to mind. Azra would hush her many times, but she ignored him. The game was being played at all the tables with intense interest until a shrill and wail broke everyone's reverie. Toby cried, "Checkmate!" and jumped with joy. Jay was holding his head in his hands in disbelief. Gina was skeptical and had her own reasoning over this loss, but she went about the business of managing the orders and keeping notes in her notebook.

A quick break was had wherein orders were refreshed, and players took a breather. All the while, they were trying to rewind their strategies with either their opponents or their coach. Azra was busy noting down the timings of each player, Toby was gloating about winning, and Gina was watching Jay eye her with delight. She found it very interesting. Soon the players had another rematch with their opponents.

This time, Jay would eye Toby with a smile that exhibited dimples on both sides of his cheeks as she would play and then would go into deep thought when it was his turn to move. At one point, he took a good three minutes to tap the clock, and Gina was fuming over it. Jay noticed his cousin's desperation and chose to ignore it while continuing to play.

This time before Toby could squeal on her 'checkmate' announcement, Gina made a proclamation, "And here we go again!" She covered her ears and moved her eyeballs upward.

Jay was undisturbed and placid, but Azra looked at their timings and could not contain himself. "What's got into you, Jay? I thought you were better than that?"

Instead, Jay just shrugged his shoulders and looked at Toby, who was jumping with joy despite the stilettos she was wearing.

Soon the club dispersed, and while the two were busy cleaning, Antonio came about with his batch of supplies for the next day. The café was awfully quiet except for Yogi's woofs now and then.

Finally, Jay broke the silence. "Are you okay?"

"Sure!" Gina was quick to respond as if she were waiting to ask this question, "Why shouldn't I be? It was you who was losing against that blonde. Not me," she stated in a dry tone while scrubbing the pots.

Jay chuckled. "Sure! That blonde and me. By the way, that blonde had a name. Toby," he said in a defensive tone. "I admit I was losing on purpose. But I enjoyed it immensely."

There was silence for a bit, and Gina finally said, "Go on. Explain your actions," she demanded, turning off the faucet and facing him.

"I liked her innocence in that squeal. She had so much to offer."

"Offer?" asked a confused Gina with a frown. "I wish she could offer ear plugs!" she stated in a sarcastic tone.

Jay laughed and clarified, "Gina, I admit that screech was irritating, but she was doing it with no inhibitions. She was who she is."

Gina was totally confused. "Is that infatuation that is doing the talking?"

"No! No," he said out loud, trying to again make a point, but she just nodded her head in dismay and went back to cleaning.

Before locking up the café, he asked her, "Dinner?"

"Don't bother. Just come home. I have plenty of food."

# CHAPTER EIGHT

*"Reality continues to ruin my life."* — **Bill Watterson**

The trio reached home, and soon the cousins were sitting at the dining table. Gina could not end the conversation with him having the last word over somebody's analysis. After all, her soon-to-be profession had to say the last word, so she blurted, "You know..." she played with the spoon on her plate, "Toby is definitely not a mature individual."

Jay eyed her with arched eyebrows and groaned. "I do realize you will be a successful psychologist, but for now, let me enjoy the moments of innocence with that girl whom you refer to as a blonde."

There was a momentary silence, but both the cousins kept looking into each other's eyes. Finally, the matter was laid to rest.

After the dishes were done and the kitchen was rendered spotless, they sat in the living room with their notebooks. Jay was calculating his expenses and profits for the day while Gina was making notes.

"So, I have made the bookings for Yogi and me." He tried to sound enthusiastic. "We leave next Monday morning for Los Angeles, catch the cruise from there, and will return the following Monday."

"Oh good!" she said in a pleasing tone. "So which islands will you be touring? And what is the name of the cruise?"

"It's the Pacific Cruise Line, and we will be taking a tour of the North Pacific islands."

"So, like Hawaii?" she sounded very excited this time as she shut her diary to get his attention.

"Yes, the itinerary says we will stop at Oahu and the big island."

"Cool! This change will be good for you. I don't remember you ever having gone on a holiday since Sasha left you," she asked in an earnest tone.

"She took away all my thunder," he muttered.

There was an awkward silence filling the room, and that made Gina uncomfortable. She was about to get up when Jay said in an earnest tone, "Thanks, Gina. I really appreciate your time at my place. I could not have found any better substitute to look after my café and home."

She acknowledged, "Sure thing. I have ways to get you back," she said with a wink. "By the way, you might want to sign a power of attorney over to me and date it."

"Wow, you are so meticulous." He was impressed and promised to follow up on this.

"By the way, I have given you as my emergency contact on the cruise form," he said in a casual tone to which she just shrugged her shoulders expressing a 'whatever' attitude.

*Little did she know that this would turn out to be meaningful in the days to come!*

The night was another peaceful affair. Jay slept well. They woke up chirpy and to a *woof-woof* morning. After the master and Yogi's usual run around the block, he started to brew coffee.

# CHAPTER NINE

*"Life is like riding a bicycle. To keep your balance, you must keep moving."* — **Albert Einstein**

"Coffee!"

"No thanks, I have my tea bags and supplies," she replied. "So, what's tonight?"

"Oh, you will love it. In fact, you will have many people to study given your specialization." He was quick to respond with laughter. She frowned.

"It's talent night, and about ten people have signed up, and five are on a waiting list. I'm pretty sure the ones on the waiting list will have to give their performance next week." He showed her the diary where he kept the log.

"Aha," she exclaimed, peeping into it. "So, tell me how I will make bookings for the coming week."

"You will see tonight. They rush to perform. Ten dollars for each performance, though."

"Got it, boss," she teased.

While Jay took a shower, Yogi was hanging around with Gina who chose to browse through the guide on the television while preparing her lavish breakfast.

"Yummy! That smells so good. What you cooking?" he inquired sniffing around while pouring breakfast for his pet in his bowl.

"Come join me! There's plenty for both of us," she said with fervor, adding with pride, "I have made eggs and sausages with toast."

He loved what he saw and could not resist, but then he was quick to decline the offer and barge into his room.

Gina gave out a sigh, and after a few nods, came to terms with him and his actions. "I wish he would forget the past," she muttered out loud.

After a while when Jay was leaving for work, he saw Gina nicely settled down in front of the television with her breakfast.

He smiled. "Will see you then?"

"Sure thing," she said nonchalantly.

**********

The day at the café was the same as any other day. Same crowd, however, Gina was looking forward to that peculiar knock by that lady in robes, the sunset where she could connect with her past, and then the talent show Jay, for once, was excited about.

The clock struck seven, and all kinds of people started pouring in. She liked the assortment of the crowd and got busy observing each of their expressions. There were spectators and performers. She could easily distinguish between them by their state of nervousness and impatience.

Jay was holding a list in one hand while clutching a microphone with the other. He looked totally in control for someone who was going to master the ceremony. Once he made sure all had their drinks, he started the show with reading the rules first.

"The winner will get a gift card from my store," he declared before calling out the first performer's name.

"Hi, I'm Caleb," he said with confidence. "I am a recent high school graduate and would like to dedicate this poem to my dear friend, Aria, for whom I'm ready to risk it all," he said, pointing toward a young lady.

Suddenly, all the eyes were on this young lady who was sipping from her cup. When she felt the heat from all the glances, she promptly put down her drink and nodded elegantly with a wave. She was blushing, and Gina felt a surge of excitement seeing that reaction.

*"We met as strangers in the dark corridors where only the lockers existed.*

*"It started off with my book accidentally falling, and you happened to be around to pick it up for me with that smile and a mere 'thank you from my end.'*

*"Was just like anybody would say to anyone.*

*"Hours ticked by, and we met again.*

*"History repeated itself in the hallway.*

*"Psychology book falling.*

*"You coming to my rescue.*

*"This time our eyes met.*

*"A deeper smile said it all.*

*"Days turned into months, and we were ready to take the next step.*

*"To shape our destiny with each other's company.*

*"Today we have graduated, and before we go on our respective paths,*

*"I proclaim my adoration for you and have a simple query?"*

All foreheads frowned including hers.

*"Can we take it to the next level?"*

Before Aria could respond, the shouts of "Yes-Yes-Yes" from the audience had filled the café. She chose to look down, turning pink with all the adulation.

Gina was bothered more about her cousin at that time than analyzing Aria as a psychologist and crossed her fingers while eyeing him. Jay took a few minutes to come up on the stage as he had a hard time to find words to describe his creation.

"Love is tough. Love is betrayal. Love can be treacherous. My conclusion is don't waste your time over it," he said with an acerbic tone. His responses made everyone, including the composer, go wide-eyed. He realized and changed tables by going softer, "Kids, you both have long ways to go. Why bind yourself to each other at this junction? Go explore," he tried to droll.

The stillness seemed to denote that not everyone agreed with him. Gina noticed it all, but without acting on it, just chose to absorb it silently.

"All right, moving on to the next participant..." Jay introduced another performer who was there to play his harmonica. The audience was in awe as he performed, and that was followed by a thunderous applause from everyone present, including Jay and Gina. The night was rolling along fine after that as high schoolers, and young and middle-aged adults showed off their talent in magic, playing a flute, juggling of hats, playing cards, and balancing of the bamboo sticks. Gina found it weird but was equally elated. Then there was the last and final performance for the evening. She was a unique performer. She was blind and could identify any sound that the audience made. That made her the star of the show for the evening as everyone voted for her to get the gift card.

The evening ended with all the performers on the stage and a big applause and bow for them as they exited the café. Gina was quick to get hold of Caleb who was hanging around with Aria. She introduced herself as an assistant to

Jay in that café and wished the couple the best for their future. That touched them, and Aria was quick to hug her. Jay noticed all this from a distance but kept quiet.

Cleaning and restocking started when these two cousins were by themselves. This time Gina could not keep it to herself. "You were harsh," she stated.

"Excuse me?" He was loud as if taking out his anger in those two words.

His reaction prompted her to come directly to the point. "Just because love was not good for you, doesn't mean it will be bad for others as well. You don't go about giving love a bad name!"

"Ha-ha! You're talking as if love is a noun."

"Isn't it?"

He paused for a bit, then nodded. "Listen, it's my duty to guide these high school students. After all, what's the old expression 'once bitten twice shy?'"

"Not necessarily. There is a 'happily-ever-after' too," she said in an angry voice while scrutinizing him. He avoided her gaze and pretended to be busy cleaning. Gina gave out a cold sigh and tried to get his attention by being caring and sympathetic. "Let go of your past. Trust me, you will find happiness thereafter."

He paused at what he was doing. Then he faced her and questioned candidly, "How do you know? You are not in a relationship, and you still look out at the sunset each day."

"Yes, you are correct. I cannot let go of my past. But then I do dare to visit it each day. When something reminds you of your past, you get extremely angry. And as for me being in a relationship, I have not yet found anyone special, but I am open to it," she said with a twinkle in her eyes.

Jay wanted to comment further but was interrupted by the delivery for the next day. Soon it was closing time, and they decided to meet at home. Dinner was a casual affair, and while they were hanging in the family room, Jay's phone beeped. Gina was very curious to see the text. It was his mom.

**Jay's Mom**: *Heard you are going on a vacation. Very happy for you :)*

Gina blushed and was on pins and needles since she knew her cousin would not refrain from cussing. She was quick to mumble "good night"and rushed to her bedroom. Jay was busy with his numbers, so he did not hear any of it.

Once satisfied with the figures, he looked up and saw Gina had disappeared while his phone was blinking. He frowned and reached for it. At first, he had a gentle smile that was followed by a frown. He immediately got up and gently knocked on her bedroom door.

Gina was prepared. She gingerly replied, "Come in."

After pushing the door open, he asked, "Did you tell my mom about my trip?" he inquired in a combatant voice.

She kept her cool and pretended everything was normal. "Aha," as she continued to scribble in her journal.

"May I ask, why?" he demanded, standing across the bed from where she was sitting.

"Well, she is my guardian, and she ought to know my whereabouts. I informed her that I will be here for more time than originally planned. She asked why? I had to give her the facts." She shrugged her shoulder and then pretended to get busy while still aware of his presence.

He kept quiet since he was confused and did not know what to argue next. In the meantime, Gina's heart kept fluttering like a butterfly. The lull in the air was panicking her, and she needed closure, pushing her to peep through her glasses and ask in a very informal tone, "Anything else?"

Jay was still staring at the text contemplating how to respond and was lost deep in thought. Gina's questioning made him come out of his trance. "No, I'm just wondering how I should respond to her. It's been ages since I have communicated with her, so I'm a little uncomfortable to respond," he flushed.

"Ages?" she questioned.

Her raised voice made his heart skip a beat as he gulped and nodded in acknowledgment.

"She is your mother for goddamn sake. Your blood. I'm yearning for such a connection with my blood. Count your blessings, Jay," she scorned at him.

There was stillness in the air.

Gina took a few deep breaths to calm down and then asked in an unreserved manner, "So, there is no interaction at all between you two?"

"She keeps inquiring about my welfare every other day, but I just respond with an okay," he said honestly.

She was devastated. Tears were trickling down her cheeks she was so angry. She wanted to slap him, beg him, and shake him up all at the same time to make him come to his senses, but alas, it will only make matters worse.

Quickly wiping her tears, she responded crudely, "Even now, you can respond in one word. No need for a sentence." She frowned and continued, "The word 'thanks' will do."

Jay quietly left her room.

********

Around midnight, Gina woke up startled to the constant barking of Yogi, which was followed by a lot of commotion. She could hear the wood creak courtesy of the wooden homes in California along with the whimpers of Jay. It got her very curious. She was quick to get out of her bed and walk toward his room. She turned on the light prior to gently knocking his door and then barged in. She was appalled to see Yogi in the arms of his owner, and the shadow falling on Jay making him look very fearful and shaken. She was quick to turn on the lights of his room. Jay was sweaty, terrified, and shivering.

"Are you okay? What happened?" she inquired in a concerned tone.

Jay was still trying to get over the nightmare, and the lights in his room made him sightless for a bit. He breathed in and then exclaimed, "All because of you," he accused her.

She was confused and also angry but kept her composure by placing her hands on her hips with a body language which was asking for an explanation. "We called it a night talking about my past, and that resulted in this darn nightmare of me drowning and a voice pleading to go on in the background," he grumbled while still holding Yogi, who was licking his face.

She was quick to sit on his bed and kept her hand on his knee while gently stroking it.

"Jay, please embrace your past," she said in a gentle tone. "The more you shield yourself, the more it will bully you."

He refused to discuss it further, so she chose to keep quiet. Seeing his helpless expression, Gina felt sorry for him and apologized.

He was quick to nod at that, and whispered, "It's all right," in a childlike manner.

Then he lay down into a curled position while continuing to hug Yogi. Gina had moist eyes and felt so helpless seeing him like this. She covered him with a blanket and walked out of his bedroom while switching off the lights. After closing the door behind her, she chose to sit on the couch in the family room.

This time her eyes gave away, and tears were falling down her cheeks. She let them flow as her mind wandered to the years when he was her best pal after the demise of her parents. She recollected how he would wander around her to always cheer her up. Those goofy faces he would make just to make her smile. If she would be crying, he would also give her his toys to play with.

She snickered on an incident when he fought with his school friends when they made fun of her height. Those loving hugs were unforgettable, but then she also recalled her fights with him. All those memories made her laugh and cry at the same time. "He is the best brother I could ask for. Alas, I can't help him now." She pondered over the question for a bit before answering it on her own. "Well, I have made him my object of research with the hopes to help heal him. What more can I do?" she questioned, wiping her tears, but she was not convinced. She continued to sit there somber and upset.

**********

Dawn came in with a wink of an eye, and Yogi broke her sleep, moistening her cheeks. She was quick to open her eyes and realized she had dozed off on the couch.

"Good morning," Jay chirped while making his cup of joe. "What happened, why are you sleeping here?"

Gina had half a mind to say *'courtesy of you,'* but she chose to be quiet and continued preparing her cup of strong tea by dipping three tea bags in her cup.

"Did you sleep well?" she inquired stirring the cup after adding her desired fat-content milk and sat opposite him while crossing her legs on the chair.

He nodded assertively sipping his coffee. "Susan mentioned that such episodes will soon be gone, but I fail to understand why they recur now and then," he said, casually munching his almond cookie. "Although the episodes have drastically decreased they still manage to prevent me to live a normal life." He winked with moist eyes.

She glared at him first, then to ease the mood, she asked, "What?" But she was quick to put her cup down. "You're still seeing that shrink?"

"Yes, these nightmares disturb me," Jay defended himself after a quick gulp.

"Sure, they would bother me, too," she justified to him. "What I admire is that you have continued to reach out for help."

At first, Jay chose not to respond but then opened up. "Those aches and pains in my back and headaches were taking a toll on me due to those continuous nightmares. I had to reach out, and since I saw changes happening, I decided to continue to see her. In fact, Yogi is in my life courtesy her, and even the idea of making a bucket list is thanks to her. I have a goal to live for each day." He grinned, looking at his buddy, who was eating from his bowl.

He realized he had opened up too much, so he tried to change the subject. "You do realize that by calling my therapist a shrink, you're addressing yourself with that name, right?" He force-laughed over it.

She turned up her nose over that remark and continued to sip her beverage.

"So, what was the diagnosis?" she inquired in a pragmatic tone.

"Some weird acronym." He shrugged his shoulders while rolling his eyes. "A jargon that will make me forget my ABCs." He snickered.

There was a pause. "But before you come to any conclusions, this thingy was caught very early on, and my symptoms were elementary. So no medication was prescribed." Then with his eyes toward his cup, he continued, "Although I admit I was bored to death by these counseling sessions that consisted of short- term, goal-oriented psychotherapy where she asked me to change patterns of my living. That's when I was advised to adopt Yogi." The word made his pet immediately look at him and curve his head in adoration. Jay was quick to get up and cuddle him. "I know you are precious. I love you," he said to him in a fun and zestful manner.

Gina observed the love and the special bond they shared and could not resist. "Awww." She was quick to come and sit next to them.

"I'm glad you reached out for help. The last time I was here, you were stuck in your past and refused to move forward even though you had planned out your bucket list. This adoption has inspired you to think of your future and inspires you to keep marching toward your goals," she said in a sincere tone. "And I am glad you were not prescribed anything. Phew," she said arching her eyebrows, showing her creases on her forehead.

"Well, she has been stressing the same thing as me. Let go! Don't dwell on your past. Susan and I analyzed my past, and she gave me exercises to cross-examine them often. Yada yada," he said, shrugging his shoulders. He reached out for his cup on the table, continuing to sip his drink on the floor next to his dog.

She listened to him, and then her expertise spoke, "You know..." she said, pulling up her index finger and waving it to stress a point, "... you should go on a retreat where it's just you. The day-to-day activities can bog down anybody not allowing you to focus within. Let your mind and heart sync completely."

He grinned walking toward the backyard eyeing his pet.

"What?" she asked in a furious tone.

"I can't believe my once-annoying cousin has become so intelligent," he teased her. She scrunched her nose and walked toward the backyard to see what Yogi was up to. He was digging ruthlessly.

Jay followed her, and as they both observed the pet, she said, "Take it easy today. Since I'm here, you have the luxury to do so. Let me handle the store, you rest." She sounded so motherly that for once, his heart melted. It could be seen in his eyes that they had softened, and he was wearing that gentle and appreciative smile. But, alas, that was only for a few minutes. It wore off immediately, and he was quick to say no.

She nodded her head in disbelief and breathed out a loud, cold sigh but could not resist giving him a smack on his back with her hand. His pet was quick to woof at her.

That alarmed her, making her take a few steps back quickly, while Jay was quick to pat Yogi. "Atta boy." He was very proud of the fact that he is protective of him and could not miss adding, "No wonder Susan asked me to get a pet." He chuckled and winked at Gina. She was quick to raise her eyebrows with a 'whatever' attitude.

# CHAPTER TEN

*"Life isn't about finding yourself. Life is about creating yourself."* — **George Bernard Shaw**

The day was the usual when Gina walked in the store. She gave a quick glance to the blackboard and uttered loudly, "Aha, it's painting night tonight. How exciting, although I haven't painted since I finished elementary school." She chuckled over it, struggling to put on her apron.

Jay was quick to add, "But believe me, Gina, you will get to painting in just one session. Diana is a wonderful moderator and coach. I enjoy it every time," and then he inquired if she would like to participate this evening.

"*What!* Are you serious? Didn't you just hear me?" she said irritatingly, pouring a cup of tea for herself. "I have *never* painted before. I know you just want to put me in the spotlight and then make fun of me, huh?" she said while being angry and resentful about it.

Jay was quite calm. "Trust me, you will enjoy it tremendously. She will instruct you from the beginning. It's like holding a book *Painting for Dummies* and getting practical knowledge from it."

But that did not convince her, and she gave out a snicker. "What do you mean? Will she teach me to hold a brush, draw the outline, and help to choose the colors to paint with?" She mocked later over it, "Seriously, does she have that much patience?"

Jay paused and looked straight at her. "Look, I know why you are so upset with me? I get it, okay? I am still not comfortable letting someone walk my terrain."

"When will you be? When will you let others come close to you?" She moved her arms in the air to show her frustration.

He let out a cool sigh. "Maybe once I'm back from my trip." Then he smiled. "You said this 'alone' time will help me embrace my past and move on."

"Well, it's high time, Jay. Because you need to start depending on people around you and not just that pet of yours," she said, shaking her head back and forth to show how frustrated she was.

He just chuckled at her reaction.

"So, maybe this is a yes, then?" he asked, squinting his eyes and then added her name to the diary while pulling out ten dollars from the box and placing it in a big brown envelope marked 'Painting Night.' "You know there are perks to knowing the owner since I have heard there is a waiting line just to get in. You have been bumped up." He grinned. She just nodded but was not really convinced how the evening will unfold for her.

The sunset and that masked lady whose eyes would always be intriguing were the highlights of the day until an old lady with red spectacles and gray hair walked in with a rolling cart.

"Hello," she chirped like a bird waving at Jay, who was quick to reciprocate.

"Diana, meet my cousin, Gina. Gina, meet Diana, the moderator and coordinator this evening."

Diana had arrived early allowing her to arrange the tables and chairs individually. Jay handed the cash register to Gina while he went ahead to help putting up the easels after laying paper tablecloths over eight tables.

"Wait. Jay, don't we have just seven participants each evening? Why do we need the eighth table?" Diana inquired, pulling things out of her rolling suitcase.

"Diana, my cousin will be joining, too," Jay said exhibiting the dimple on his cheek.

"With that indention in your cheek, how can I say no?" Diana said with a cold sigh.

He blushed and became embarrassed, simply pretending to get busy.

Gina giggled but soon came to the point. "Diana, I have no experience at all painting. Can I still be a suitable candidate?" She raised her voice and inquired while she was arranging the eats for the evening.

"Sure, hon! Although I'm glad you informed me now." She pulled the white strands of hair behind her ear, which made the half dozen trinkets on her wrist tinkle.

"Oh, I love your bracelets," Gina stared at them with elation.

"I made these. You like them?" Diana looked proud and happy. "I even conduct classes on how to make these. However, the venue is different."

"Now, that's one class I would readily register for." Gina eyed her cousin. He avoided her.

The clock struck seven, and Jay got ready behind the cash register to get that clink going. He enjoyed the ka-ching sound and at times wondered what it would be like to have dreams of just this sound. He realized he was wearing a smile over this thought, and Gina, who was always eyeing him, could not resist. "Aha! You already excited about this class?"

He avoided her again.

Once everybody had settled in with their drinks and eats, the class was in session.

"Today, we are going to paint something about your yesteryears, your past." Jay was not happy hearing that. Gina just nodded her head in disbelief. *"Can this day get any worse than this?"* she muttered. *"Why is life throwing cannonballs?"*

She fretted, arching her eyebrows as if they could touch the bangs of her hair.

She asked for clarification and then brooded. "But, Diana, I just can't draw."

"No worries, hon. Just describe your memory, and I will render it. All you need to do is fill it in with colors." She smiled, showing off her tea-stained teeth.

Jay was taking deep breaths while keeping the knots on his forehead in check as if the focus on his breath brought him answers and gave him insight.

Gina was nervous since she was okay to say bye and hi to the sunsets that exhibited so many memories for her, but to actually put them on paper, she was not sure.

Seeing the confusion in the group, Diana clarified, "It could be a picture of you playing with your dog or you being cuddled with your parents on the bed or you with a bunch of friends at a birthday party or maybe visiting a garden or a favorite place. Anything! And the beauty of this style of painting is that you don't have to be specific. It can be abstract."

"But I don't understand why this style of painting?" Jay protested. "Why not just paint mountains and oceans and a house around it. Let's keep it simple like we always have."

He realized and clarified with a smile, "Actually, such kinds of paintings have inspired me to buy a beach house. Soon," he said, scratching his earlobe while being conscious to continue to wear that smile.

"I understand what you are getting at, Jay," Diana said. "But you guys have been in my class now for over three weeks. I want more than landscapes from you. A change in style of painting and surrealism is a modern painting style that juxtaposes various images together to give a startling effect. The images that some of you might ask me to draw would be illogical and could have a dream-like quality, but that's what emphasizes your subconscious."

"Wow," exclaimed one attendee of the class. "I can't wait to get started." She giggled while pondering this.

That was followed by a couple of more nods, which forced Gina and Jay to tag along but with a sulk.

"So which painters have used this kind of style?" an enthusiastic participant asked inquisitively.

Walking around the room with her tablet, Diana was happy to give examples and showed some famous paintings of painters like Frida Kahlo, her surrealist self-portraits depicting her intense emotional and physical pain. Some other painters included Joan Miro, Toyen, Valentine Hugo, and Jean Hugo. It gave the students an idea of what to look for within while also getting some of them excited.

Jay was fidgeting with his pen, eyeing his paper, and trying to draw some ideas. Just then, he muttered, "I'm out of ideas. I quit." He got up from his assigned table and walked away.

Diana was surprised at first, but then shrugged her shoulders and let it go. Jay got behind his counter and pretended to be busy. She walked casually toward him and whispered, "You know, I can always help you if you just give me an idea of your thoughts. All you have to do is peek into your past and let me know, hon," she said with a gentle smile.

"It's the past that I cannot embrace," he said in a sharp tone that caught Gina's attention while she was making notes of her favorite memories with her parents in that huge car of theirs.

The tone cautioned Diana to step back. "As you please," she responded and went toward the other tables.

Gina got a one-on-one consultation with Diana, who gave a tutorial on colors, shapes, and lines as she helped them arrange in a harmonious correlation depending on her thoughts, and soon this to-be psychologist was in a world of colors and tone while keeping the rhythm. These frequent pauses allowed her creative force to intervene and add new creations of form, melody, and coloration using acrylic paint since it was a much easier than using oil paints.

Diana had outlined her memory with a vivid sketch that registered strongly in her mind. The wheels portrayed the car, and the three figures in it were delicately outlined as the dad, the mom, and a child. The scenery was of a cave that was one of her favorite places she had often visited with her parents, the Robber's Cave in Dehradun, India. While giving a touch of brown and earthen colors to the caves that were broken into two halves by Mother Nature, she gave blue color to the ground as the river flowed. While painting, she had some mixed emotions.

At times, she would feel happy, which would give her goosebumps and even moist eyes. The next second, she was melancholic, which would make her pause with the energy in her body draining her. All of this was giving her the chills as the temperature of her physical self was alternating too soon. She was confused at first and paused to get her sweatshirt. Once warm with the layers, she realized her mind was restless, and that made her breathe fast and deep to get oxygen in her lungs. Amidst all this, she continued to paint, and midway through, she found herself relaxing and eventually humming to the background music of the café.

The attendees took a break for refreshments, but Gina continued with zeal. Jay observed all this, and at first envied her for giving in so easily, but eventually became inspired.

With just thirty minutes left before the class ended, Jay approached Diana in a humble tone, "I think I know what I want to express."

"Oh sure, I will be happy to help you. Give it to me in words, and maybe I can help sketch it out for you."

"A monk," Jay said.

"Oh, dear, you will be another Jean Hugo," she exclaimed loudly and everyone paused.

"Err... what do you mean?" he inquired, confused with a frown.

She was quick to look for Saint Valentine from Jean Hugo on Google and show it to him.

"Look, this is the painting done by this artist. History repeats."

She grinned.

He frowned further.

As his instructor got busy outlining it for him on his blank canvas, he sat there staring at those lines she was etching. Unknowingly, tears started flowing down his cheeks, and he was unaware until Diana inquired, "Are you okay?"

He looked at her, and that's when he realized his heavy eyelids. He blinked a couple of times to let go of the water and was quick to wipe the fluid off his cheeks with his full-sleeved shirt.

Silence can be interpreted in many ways. He chose to let her make her own conclusions since he had plenty to fight with at the moment.

After a few stares at him, she got back to outlining, and in a few minutes, she declared, "Here, it's all ready. Now you can either choose to paint it with oil or acrylic. It's entirely your choice. The paints are over there. Go help yourself."

He sat there staring at it while she went around the café to check on the others. The canvas was echoing peace and serenity, and he became further confused. "How could you be at peace after giving away everything, huh?"

Gina placed a gentle hand on his shoulder, and that got him out of his reverie. He blinked a couple of times to come back to the present, then looked at her. "How could it be? How could he be so peaceful leaving his blood behind?"

Gina patted his back continuously. "I'm so proud of you to take this leap," she said with pride.

He had no emotions since he was very confused.

"All right, so we have only a few minutes left before we wrap up this class. Those of you who have not finished can register yourself for the next class," Diana announced. "Jay, I think you'll have to finish this at the next class. I will have to pack up."

Jay was quick to nod. "No worries, I have an eternity to finish this painting."

"Excuse me!" she sounded confused.

Gina interrupted, "Ha-ha.... He meant it could take forever for him to finish since he is leaving for his holiday this coming Monday." She gulped while brushing her bangs nervously.

"Oh, you're going on a holiday?" screeched Diana. "It's high time!" She clapped her hands in glee. "So, will you be taking care of the store in his absence?" she asked Gina to which she was quick to nod.

"Yes, it's only a week. I can do that." She shrugged her shoulders and continued, "Running this café has always been my dream, so why miss this chance?" She winked at Jay, who raised his eyebrows instead.

Soon the attendees started leaving. Some registered for the next class including the cheery Gina, who had had the experience of going on a roller coaster ride of emotions during the class. When Diana had announced the end of the class, this pygmy could not believe where the time flew. She had never felt so grounded in her life since she could actually be the witness of her sorrows and happiness at the same time charting it on a canvas with colors. The painting was partially done, but by the looks of it, she had explained it to such an extent that onlookers could get a peek into the state of her conscience. Gina felt proud and thanked Diana while promising to meet her at the next class.

"Sure, hon." She waved at her, allowing her bracelets to jingle along.

Jay chose to keep his canvas with him. He took it to the back room and put it in a safe place.

While Gina started to clean up, he took his time to go back out.

"Finally!" she said teasingly, mocking him all the while. "I thought I might have to clean up by myself tonight." At first, he adjusted his hair, then chuckled and went about helping his cousin.

This time neither of them talked, whined, or complained. They both were busy in their own worlds because each of them was having a conversation with their mind and heart. Occasional woofs from Yogi would make them exchange a few dialogues, but then their individual minds and hearts would take over.

Dinner was also a quiet affair. They both chose to retire early. Gina was self-absorbed in her own world that she did not care to pen down the day regarding her object of research. Sleep came easy for Jay, and what was even more surprising for him was that the alarm clock woke him up the next day.

# CHAPTER ELEVEN

*"You cannot find peace by avoiding life."* — **Michael Cunningham**

A chirpy good morning was exchanged as the two cousins sat down with their respective beverages.

"How was your night?" asked a curious Gina.

"Surprisingly, it was very peaceful." Jay nodded, twisting one part of his lip down. "I must say as peaceful as that canvas Diana etched for me."

"Wow."

"Maybe I should actually color that canvas for a peaceful ever after." Jay arched his eyebrows, and Gina gave her approval by showing thumbs up.

When Jay came out from his shower, the appetizing aroma of fresh pancakes and eggs teased him to an extent he couldn't resist and ended up grabbing a plate. Gina was ecstatic beyond words. It was like someone finally acknowledging and accepting her invitation for a meal.

She was brisk and quickly placed the cooked food on the stove to a plate. Carrying the plate around with her, she headed to the refrigerator to gather the syrup before grabbing the cutlery with the same hand and rushing to the table. While pushing the drawer in with her hips, the fork fell on the tiled kitchen giving off a chink sound. Yogi was quick to come in and started sniffing that area with the hope of being able to grab some morsels of food.

Jay got up abruptly to help. "Slow down," he urged, grabbing the plate from her. She took a breather, and soon she sat next to him with her plate of food.

"I was thinking of hiring help for you," he declared. "I just saw your efficiency." He chuckled, putting a morsel of pancake in his mouth.

"What me? No. No. You have not seen my brilliance!" She revolted with a knife in one hand and a fork in the other, banging the table gently with it.

"Now, you are acting like a kid, Gina." He arched his eyebrows. "Look, I want you to continue with your research along with managing my store. Don't want you to be slogging over it," he spoke in a realistic tone.

"Now with that frame of mind... yes, I shall take up this offer. So, do you have anyone in mind?"

"Yes... Samuel."

"What?" she shrieked. "No way, I'd rather be toiling alone," she protested.

He paused in between his bites and asked with a frown and looking genuine, "Why not?"

She, in turn, scrunched her nose. "He walks and talks like a duck!"

Jay paused for a bit and then burst into laughter. "I like how you have been checking him out. But honestly, he is not an aquatic bird. He is just an individual like you and me. We all have our personal issues. He has issues with his weight since he loves to eat."

Gina was embarrassed and clarified, "I understand where you are going with this. But honestly, when I came to visit you two years ago, he was bulkier than what he is now." She paused for a while before continuing, "I think he has lost weight." She chuckled and quickly changed the topic. "More pancakes?"

Jay eyed her while giving out a sly smile and then waved his hand and head in unison to indicate a negative. She gave a quick glance at him and then called out to Yogi with the pretense of patting him.

Jay didn't give up on that topic easily. He went on. "Yes, we all grow over time, and he is not the same," he asserted, getting up from the table and cleaning up. "I will ping Samuel to come by today, and we can discuss this more."

At first, Gina pretended to play with her food, then she shrugged her shoulders to denote an okay.

"Great! See you at the café, then."

# CHAPTER TWELVE

*"If my life is going to mean anything, I have to live it myself."*
**— Rick Riordan**

Once Gina was alone, she quickly pulled out her phone to check her 'Whatsapp' contacts. Samuel was one of them. She checked out his profile picture, which had him in this awkward pose that exhibited his paunch. *Eww! Why can't he suck it in for a picture?* She went on to check her previous messages exchanged with him that mostly involved hilarious forwarded texts and a few queries now and then. She noticed she had responded only to a handful. She gave out a sinuous smile, followed by a blush recollecting those lanky fingers, an impassioned smile exhibiting his crooked but white teeth when he would go out of his way to help her in the store during her last visit.

"Jeez, I'll get to see all this again." She rolled her eyes while wrapping herself with her arms and felt goosebumps of anxiety. She was a wreck as one moment she was biting her lips in anxiety, and the next moment her eyes blinked continuously, and in another moment, she would breathe rapidly while her heart fluttered like a butterfly in anticipation. The sudden change of emotions was exhausting her, and she realized it soon enough to blow out a breath which made her slouch.

She felt relaxed for a bit. "I have to keep a check on my composure since this time Jay will not be around as a distraction." Then while sipping her tea, she stiffened up thinking how infatuation and crushes had never been in her dictionary. For her, relationships meant something. They had to have a face value. No wonder she was apprehensive to tread on that path.

But then, after a while, she was nodding away as if in agreement with her thoughts, and involuntarily she tapped her fingers on her mug while muttering to herself, "You have seen the rougher side of life, this should be a piece of cake. Gina, let's see where it takes you." To avoid further distraction, she turned on the television to check out the local listings and got busy.

********

"You are late!" Jay was quick to comment as she dashed into the café. "Err... yes, I'm aware of that." She tried to avoid eye contact with Jay. Putting on her apron, she went about her duties while he continued to watch her. "What's up with that beret?" he asked in an inquisitive tone with a frown. "I have never seen you wear accessories."

"Err..." She was quick to place her hand over her head to adjust it. "Don't you like it?" she asked while feeling edgy about it.

"No. Umm, I mean yes. It's just that I have never seen you wear one."

That made Gina cheerful. "Oh, thank you." And she got busy while giving a quick glance to the blackboard.

"Clay night!" She could not resist a frown.

"Yup."

"You will be surprised at the kind of customers we have. I will have to check if this young girl has registered. She is just marvelous and makes others' work bland."

That got Gina curious. "You have me intrigued. Tell me more."

He was quick to peek into that book. "Oh yes, she is registered. You will love her," he exclaimed while still eyeing the list of attendees for the evening. "Hey, I didn't know that. Samuel is coming in tonight. I think it's his first."

Gina stiffened up for a bit, then taking slow, deep breaths, she seemed to relax. "So, tell me about this girl."

"Let's keep that element of surprise for the evening. Shall we?" Jay winked and continued to clink the register with customers coming in.

Most of the day was a normal day, including the knock on the window, Jay rushing with his order, and Gina eyeing her from a distance. "You know you ought to introduce me to her, right?" She hesitated at first, then continued, "In a few days, I will be serving her."

"Oh, sure, I will. You know I never want to miss a chance to lose my customer." He chuckled, trying to arrange the tables for the evening.

"Customer?" she frowned. "But I have never seen her pay you?" She did not hesitate to inquire.

Jay paused over that query. "Oh, Gina, she has paid me for her lifetime in bulk," he said in a pensive tone, blinking a couple of times, and then got back to his work.

She frowned further and wanted more, but just then her eyes met with someone at the door. Her heart started to race, and her eyes began to flicker. She turned around adjusting her beret.

"Hi, there!"

The voice was so near that she rolled her eyes for a bit and turned around. "Hey, you," she said, trying to be cool and unaffected by his presence.

"Where have you been all this time?" she inquired in a by-the-way tone while feigning to be busy.

Sam's eyes widened upon hearing that and was tempted to say, "You missed me?" but instead uttered, "I thought you needed time to adjust so kept myself busy," he said in an earnest tone while eyeing her moves that were not very smooth.

"Hey, there you are," cheered Jay, entering from the kitchen with a tray. "I have a proposition for you, Sam."

"For me?" Sam got curious.

"How about you help Gina in my absence for one week starting Monday?"

"Where are you going?" Sam inquired earnestly.

"I, my friend, am going on a vacation," Jay said, straightening his spine and chinning up.

"Aha." Sam was quick to high-five him. "Your body language says you're excited," he said with a smile. "And sure, I can help in the evenings after I get off work. However," he paused and looked at Gina, "the question is if your cousin is comfortable to have me around."

Jay was quick to affirm. "Of course, I discussed this with her earlier, and she has no problem with it. Am I right?" He looked at Gina for confirmation. She displayed a nonchalant attitude as if she were calm with the whole setting and just shrugged her shoulders instead.

"Just don't stand me up! Text me if you can't make it for any reason."

"Oh, sure. Although that won't happen." His eyes twinkled, and he sounded very excited.

"Awesome! Welcome aboard, Sam. I will have the paperwork ready by tomorrow for you to sign. I will pay you by the hour once I am back from my holiday."

"Done."

"So, are you here for the clay night?" Gina inquired, placing the eats from the oven onto the tray.

"Yes, I'm very excited. I made a platter earlier, this is my second."

"A platter?" Gina burst into laughter. "What do you with it? Serve rice?" she asked mockingly.

Sam let her ridicule over it while he looked at her with admiration, and when she was finished, he admitted in a passive tone. She felt embarrassed, but he wanted her to feel comfortable, so he said in a submissive tone, "Actually, I am a good cook. You'd be surprised."

She turned pink.

*Again!*

Soon the change in temperature on her face started to bother her. She felt uneasy and awkward as if someone were turning the light bulb on and off.

*Jeez! Why am I getting so sensitive to his signals?*

"Hey, all," came a deep voice connected to a lanky figure, dark skin with glasses and curly hair walking in with a trolley, and before Jay could acknowledge her presence, Hanna was quick to order. "Could you please get that clay from the trunk of my car and park the van?" Handing over the keys to him, she began to assess the area. He was quick to follow those orders.

Gina's first reaction was *ugh, she is bossy!*

Pointing toward Samuel, she asked, "Hey, you work around here?"

"Umm..." Sam was indecisive, but she was quick to point out, "I see he did not cover the floors with a tarp. If you guys are okay to clean up after class, I am fine to proceed further."

Her words made Gina frown again. Hanna settled down at a table and played around with her curls for a bit, then pointed her finger toward Gina while expressing her thoughts loudly, "Could I have my regular, please?"

Gina chose to ignore her and continued to keep her eyes toward the cash register. "Do you work here? You must be new, huh?" Hanna was persistent, but that did not deter Gina.

Jay walked in with another trolley that had the pottery wheel and saw the friction. He apologized and was quick to get her order. Gina gave a scowling facial expression to Jay while he chose to ignore her. Soon, her students for this class started coming in, and after their orders of tea and snacks, they chose a table that had newspapers covering it. Each of them was given a ball of clay they had to knead well to remove the bubbles.

Hanna continued to give instructions while circling around the room. "Knead the clay like a loaf of bread, mold it into a ball and then slam it against a piece of plaster since it is good for absorbing moisture. Do this repeatedly until the bubbles have evaporated. If you're not sure, split the ball in half with a wire and monitor the insides. While holding the sphere of clay, press the thumb into the center of the ball, halfway to the bottom. While revolving the ball in one hand, press the walls out evenly with the thumb into the inside and the fingers on the outside."

Once done, they chose to take the molds to prepare various objects that ranged from a platter to a bowl to a picture frame or coasters. The class was busy except for a few murmurs here and there. Gina looked around curiously. At times she would cast stealthy glances at the instructor who had occupied a special chamber in her heart, but mostly her eyes were glued on Sam's table purely out of curiosity as to what he intended to make that day.

A click-clack sound was heard. "I'm sorry she is late, Hanna," came a gentle voice from the store's entrance. Hanna was quick to exclaim in excitement, "Oh, here comes my favorite student."

Gina was concentrating hard on a task in the back room. She arched her eyebrows on hearing that. "Jeez, and now she has a favorite, too," she muttered and was quick to come out of the back room.

She stood glued to the floor when she saw Hanna hug a blonde who was wearing black glasses and had a white cane in her hand. She blinked a couple of times and then approached Jay, "What's going on?" she inquired in bemusement.

"Now the fun shall begin!" he said with glee, clapping his hands. "Jenna usually takes the pottery wheel. And the kinds of things she has created so far is just out of this world."

Gina continued to keep her eyebrows arched resulting in wrinkles on her forehead. "No wonder she is her favorite, huh?"

"She is everybody's favorite, Gina. Err... I don't know about others, but I am in awe of her."

Crossing her arms and tapping her feet, she was curious and was looking forward for Jenna to amaze her. She focused on this young girl who was seated on a chair where the pottery wheel was placed. Hanna gave the clay that had been kneaded well in her hand, and then taking Jenna's hand, she placed it in the bowl of water indicating where the water is placed. After doing that, she took a backseat wanting to enjoy the show.

Jenna started coning the mass of clay, bracing it between her two palms and started squeezing upward laying it on the pottery wheel. She went back and forth until the cone shape was perfectly smooth with no bumps or wobbles. Once the clay was in a wider lump at the bottom, she started applying pressure on the sides to even it out. Her slow but subtle movements with her hands gliding along the clay were a sight to watch. Many of the mates in the café also paused from their work to observe the sight. It was like a creation happening in front of their eyes except that the creator was at a loss of her own eyesight. Life was beautiful yet was treacherous for one in that café. But then that is the irony of life, beauty comes from imperfections, and Jenna was one of them!

Once she created a piece, Jenna held it with both her hands and called out to Hanna, who was quick to answer her call tenderly, "Yes?" As if on cue, Hanna handed her a wooden knife, and Jenna was back to cleaning her piece and smoothing its surface.

"How is it?" she inquired, since she was unable to see what she was holding and yet feeling the jitters with the whispers in the room.

"Oh, it's beautiful. Just like always," Hanna asserted, gripping the clay pot that had delicate curves. "I just can't wait to glaze and fire it."

"I would love to feel the finished product," Jenna cooed as others also appreciated the work. Gina was speechless and nodded along with the others. When the others got back to their work, she walked toward Jenna and whispered a few words of encouragement to her while being in awe of her persistence. She exchanged a couple of dialogues and then ended it with a gentle tap. Jay was very curious about their talk, and when she came back to the counter, he did not hesitate to inquire.

"Oh, at first, I complimented her, and then we had some girl talk," she said with shrugged shoulders while adjusting her hair in a certain way to keep that hat on her head.

Jay was still very curious. "So how does she do it?" he asked with wide eyes that had arched his eyebrows.

"I guess it is partly talent and partly it is never to give up on one's passion." She frowned, titling her head sideways. Then she paused and could not resist, "Don't tell me you haven't spoken to her?" she asked with a forefinger upright. He hesitated to answer that.

"No way!" This time her eyes widened. "Are you serious?" she asked in bewilderment as a result of which her tone was high-pitched, and everyone looked at her. Jay was quick to rush into the kitchen while Gina, for a moment, gave a steady smile to the people in the café, and then before following Jay, muttered loudly, "I'll be back."

Jay pretended to sort the cups in the storage room. She went up to him and with her arms on her hips, "Tell me it's not true and that you were just kidding," she said, nodding her head from left to right.

"What?" he said irritatingly. "What do you want me to say?" He waved his hands in the air and walked around.

"She has been coming to your café for a long time. And you are admiring her talent. Why couldn't you go and compliment her or just say hi?" she asked in a solemn tone.

"Err... I did not want to."

"There better be a good excuse than this kiddy one," she scorned at him.

"All right... all right. I'm jealous of her," he said while blushing all over.

"Jealous?"

She took a deep breath trying to keep her composure but not for long since she slapped her forehead in an awkward manner. "You must be joking, right? What's jealousy got to do with a blind girl? She is already facing a tough life, for

God's sake!"

"No... you don't get it, Gina. I understand the plight she is undergoing for being unable to see. I feel she is lucky that she does not have to face any of her past or present."

"Ugh! Do you seriously think she would prefer not to face it? She is already swamped with darkness."

But seeing Jay's expressions, she did not want to waste more time arguing with him over this. Just when she was about to walk out to the café, she said scornfully, "I'm just thankful I am not Susan, your therapist. I would not have been able to deal with a thickheaded patient who cannot think beyond himself."

He was shocked by that statement and nodded in disagreement.

********

Hanna handed her students their fired objects from last week while collecting today's ceramics to be glazed and fired for the next class. Even as she was making a note of their work, she eyed Jay and Gina one by one. "Could you please start cleaning up, and can one of you can help put my trolley in my van?" she asked while swinging her car keys in the air.

Jay was quick to walk with a mop while Gina wore a frown and a grouchy face standing there with her arms crossed, "Why can't she do it herself?"she mumbled.

Sam heard that and was quick to walk in Hanna's direction to grab her keychain and follow the orders. There was another round of snacks and beverages devoured by the attendees before they parted ways. Jay handed a cup of beverage for Jenna to his cousin who, after a lot of back and forth arguments with her, finally gave in and approached the young blonde girl with it.

Today, the cleaning took less time since Sam stayed back to help, and that led to quite a few casual conversations between the trio.

Once back home, Gina did not have the stamina to argue over the Jenna episode.

*His baby steps toward moving ahead make me restless! I wish he took big, steady strides.* She sighed. *One can only hope!*

Finally, she decided to write it in her journal while looking forward to some pleasant days with Sam, who would be assisting her part-time.

Morning came with a blink when Jay asked for Gina's help. "I will take off for a few hours around noon if it's okay with you? I need to pick up some papers from the lawyer and also shop for a few basics."

Gina was surprised and could not resist while crunching her nose. "I thought you will just go in those rags."

"Ha-ha... you're very funny."

"By the way, tonight is karaoke night. You are welcome to sing along." He winked at her. "Today, you could showcase your bathroom singing to the world."

"Ha-ha... you seriously know how to get back to me." She eyed him with stern looks while he grabbed a fruit and left for work.

# CHAPTER THIRTEEN

*"Nobody realizes that some people expend tremendous energy merely to be normal."*
**— Albert Camus**

Evening came early since the minds were busy with chores and anticipation. Gina wanted to be in the limelight this evening more so since Sam had signed the papers to be her right-hand man for the coming week with her. At first, she was straining hard on a song that she could remember to sing well. Once she could finalize it, she put on her earplugs to listen to each high and low. Eyes shut, she was engrossed and unaware how her lips parted, while her tongue would moisten her lips now and then when she hummed the tune. She was so preoccupied with it that her head would rock from left to right, and her shoulders arched allowing her arms to move involuntarily. Jay got the hint of the song as he was observing from a distance while enjoying the visuals and chuckling over it. Yogi was locked up in the storage room so that the loud music would not upset him.

Attendees started coming, and after their individual orders of beverages, they listed the name of their songs to Jay, who made sure to write the order of their performances while looking up their lyrics and saved them in that order.

Jay was enthusiastic for the evening and did not shy away from announcing that he will begin the evening with his song. That was followed by a loud cheer. As he took the microphone, Gina was curious to know the song. Then it started:

*All my bags are packed*

*I'm ready to go*

There was silence as he began while Gina got goosebumps. She silently blessed his heart and thanked destiny for being there for him. Jay continued to sing the lyrics displayed with the music in the background.

"Oh, John Denver," crooned a few girls in the background as they swayed from left to right.

*But, I'm leavin' on a jet plane*

*Don't know when I'll be back again*

*Oh babe, I hate to go*

Gina swallowed hard upon hearing the second to the last line, but she was also happy her cousin was moving ahead in the present, hoping he embraces his past completely. Thunderous applause brought her out of her reverie, pushing her to join the bandwagon too. His performance was followed by many others. The list included songs by artists Aretha Franklin's '*Respect,*' Katy Perry's '*I Kissed a Girl,*' Salt-n-Pepa's '*Push It,*' Jazmine Sullivan's '*Bust Your Windows,*' Nat King Cole's '*Smile,*' and many others.

The café was rocking with mixed vibes as the participants were singing numbers from diverse artists. At times, their voices would croak, there was pitch inaccuracy, or words would fumble as they would skip the lyrics. But, the audience loved them in spite of all the discrepancies. Gina loved the sentiments and was encouraged to showcase her 'bathroom talent' to the world.

Jay eyed Gina, signaling her that she was next. With the music fervor in the air and after listening to all the bold and so-called talented participants, she was all geared up. She took a few sips of warm water, adjusted her hair and shirt over her jeans, and walked toward the karaoke machine. Just then, she froze seeing someone enter the café. Her heartbeats increased to such an extent that she could not hear Jay call out her name.

She continued to glance at this person whose eyes instantly met with hers, but he came to his senses when he heard her name in the background. Approaching her, he tapped her shoulder to wish her good luck. She blushed and nodded walking toward her cousin. Gina was still in a trance and had to check with Jay the song she had requested. That made him nervous at first, then he reminded her, and she blinked a couple of times to ground herself.

*What a girl wants, what a girl needs,*
*Whatever makes me happy and sets you free.*

She started the first two verses while being still and frigid, but then she saw the audience cheering. She gave out a smile and eyed Sam, who too was exhibiting appreciative body language. She blushed and then let loose. Moving freely to the music, she tried drawing in the right emotions to express the lyrics in the right way just as Christina Aguilera would do it. Within minutes, she was ending it in a solemn tune with eyes closed, grounding her body after moving her limbs and hair in all directions.

*What a girl wants, what a girl needs,*
*Whatever keeps me in your arms!*
*And I'm thanking you for being there for me.*

Jay clapped with glee. That was followed by a loud applause. Jay gave her a shoulder hug.

"All right, that ends our performers for tonight unless there are any more takers?" Jay announced.

"Aye!" came a hand.

Gina's eyes widened at first, then she mingled with the crowd. Sam came up to Jay requesting a number to which he was quick to find into his database. Those few minutes felt as if time had paused as Sam and Gina kept exchanging sly looks. In the midst of all this, Gina tried to tell him something in sign language, which he could not understand. So, he walked up to her, and they exchanged a few words but soon got so engrossed in their conversation that the surroundings of the café seemed to have melted. They kept staring at each other longingly while sharing a quip or two since both exhibited a happy expression on their faces. It felt as if just these two bodies were alive and transmitted signals while everything else around had faded somewhere in the universe.

Soon all forms came into existence when the music was on, and the saxophone started to play. Jay had accidently turned on the music without giving a head's up. But he was quick to pause, and once he got Sam's attention, the show began.

*Oh when you smilin', when you smilin'*
*The whole world smiles with you*
*Yes when you laughin', when you laughin'*
*Yes the sun come shinin' through*

That was followed by claps from the audience as Sam continued to sing. Time elapsed as the audience cheered along and smiling until the last two lines made them sentimental.

*'Cause when you're smilin'... just keep on smilin'*
*And the whole world gonna smile with you.*

"Oh, I love Louis Armstrong, and this man," Jay announced as he came up and hugged Sam for ending the note with a beautiful performance.

After another round of beverages, some people either chose to stay back while a handful called it a night. Yogi was freed from the back room. He needed petting now and then, especially since he was put in another room by himself.

"Saturdays are always the best evenings of my week," Jay revealed to Gina as they were cleaning up.

"I can see that." She showed her pearly whites. "I'm thrilled you announced your holiday to your customers."

"Announced?" He took a second to recall the song. "Ha-ha, sure thing. By the way, you were not bad yourself. I loved how you grooved along with the song. At first, I got nervous seeing you all jumpy," he admitted.

"Yes, it was my first time." Gina blushed not wanting to reveal the real reason.

"So, as you now know, all the diaries are marked with different nights. The coordinators of all evenings are aware that you are the boss while I'm away," Jay pointed out to which Gina nodded in affirmative.

Soon they headed home in their individual cars. After dinner, Gina chose to sit down in front of the idiot box with Yogi while Jay was in his room packing for his trip. Little did he realize that even the suitcase had memories making him take a hiatus now and then. After a brief pause, he patted it delicately as if assuring himself that history is not going to repeat and then finally stuffed his clothes in.

*"Please leave, Jay! I need to breathe! I am feeling suffocated in your presence."* Those were the words that made him anxious, nervous, and confused. "I just couldn't understand Sasha. I gave her everything... my body, my heart and soul,

and still she did not appreciate me," he mumbled, arranging his shirts in one corner of the bag and his shorts in the other pile.

"Gosh, these women are difficult to understand. I'm never going to be in a relationship ever," he declared, wrapping his sandals in a bag. "Although, I would love to have company besides Yogi where I can have a sensible two-way conversation," he admitted with moist eyes.

After a pause, he just embraced his present. "I'm just going to enjoy this holiday and be glad that things worked out for me, and my café shall continue to mint money in my absence." He grinned at his thoughts. Finally zipping his bag, he laid it in one corner.

"All packed," he declared on his way to the living room to see Gina cuddled up with Yogi and whimpering. One glance at the screen was enough for Jay to put two and two together!

"Can we please watch something action-packed? I just don't like these namby-pamby episodes," he admitted while taking the remote from the table and asking for permission to change the show.

Gina got cautious and was quick to wipe her tears, portraying a strong face by shrugging her shoulders. "Of course."

He changed to *White Collar,* and soon they got involved in a world of crime where Neal Caffrey is eluding the FBI agent, Peter Burke, while they both try to catch long sought-after criminals in the hopes that it will eventually buy Neal his freedom. This show had the chase, the glamor, and the New York life. It had all the ingredients to keep audiences of all ages hooked, making both the cousins watch with interest.

Before calling it a night, Jay confirmed, "Tomorrow is a late start, and we close early, too." Gina yawned but was quick to raise her two hands in the air and skip around the room to express her jubilation to which Jay chuckled. "You have never been a morning person, huh?"

Soon, they called it a night.

# CHAPTER FOURTEEN

*"Life is under no obligation to give us what we expect."* — **Margaret Mitchell**

Courtesy of a weekend morning, Sunday was a slow start since only a handful of people needed to fill themselves up with caffeine. Sam was around to absorb last-minute tips from the owner and also get comfortable around Gina, who would either show attitude or just blush. He wanted some real conversation from her unlike the last time she visited this town. He was confused with her mental outlook and wanted answers, although he admitted he was enjoying the fond looks, but now a twenty-eight-year-old man wanted to move ahead and not be kept stalling for guesses. He needed answers.

"Hey, Sam, could you take Yogi out for a break and a stroll, too, during this one week?" Jay requested.

"Sure, in fact, I can start today. Gina, would you like to join me?"

"Err..."

"Go ahead, Gina. It's relatively quiet today," Jay encouraged.

She was quick to take a bathroom break where she checked herself out in the mirror and joined Sam.

"So, how is it going?" Sam inquired.

"As good it should be," she remarked with a chuckle, then got quiet.

For the next few steps, silence accompanied them, and Sam could not take it any longer. He came to the point. "Look, Gina. I like you," he proclaimed with a straight face giving her a quick glance. She chose to walk with her head bent down with her hair falling over her face. She did not bother to tuck it behind her ear, successfully leaving Sam clueless of her expressions over his admittance. He was confused and now a little anxious.

"Hello," he badgered. "Could you please say something?"

"I like your honesty, Sam..." she continued to look down, "... but I choose to stir the pot slowly regarding these emotions since it will be my first."

"Yes, I'm aware given your past, Gina. But, I am not a procrastinator. I like to move ahead and not stall."

Gina could feel the heat on her face pushing her to keep looking down as they trod upon the footpath. She chose to be mindful of her response since she was fond of him but had her own approach toward rekindling a relationship. After a couple of blinks that helped her reason within, she faced him. "Then maybe we ought to part ways, Sam. I can't rush things. It will be asking too much from my heart."

Sam was stunned by her honesty. Now it was his turn to look at the path as he was contemplating answers from within. Gina was in no hurry to get his response since she hoped he would consider her choices and chose to walk in silence. Unfortunately, the stroll ended in no time. *Darn! Just when you want time to stretch, it tends to shorten beyond words.*

"Hey, guys! Let's have a small meeting before we close the shutters of this café tonight. I would like to brief you on some matters, although Gina has the power of attorney in my absence, and I trust her judgment." He winked at her while she nodded with an appreciative smile. The trio's meeting lasted for about thirty minutes, mostly consisting of organizing things and keeping tabs on the expenses and sales in an orderly fashion to which Gina and Sam agreed.

Some things were the usual like the sunset and the once peculiar knock. This time, Jay made sure to brief the lady in the mask about his absence while introducing Gina to her from a distance. Although she wanted to be there in person for the introduction, Jay was uptight and chose to do it his way. No doubt that made her sulk as she curled her lips together to exhibit that expression while her skin wrinkled on her forehead, but it could not be visible, thanks to her bangs.

She observed the lady's reaction from a distance. Her eyes were doing a lot of talking. They widened at first, leading to the enlargement of the pupil as if it had been dilated. They stayed in that position while she was taking time to register the announcement. Then her lips twitched and twirled as if she were inquiring. She must have a handful of questions since her pupils were also moving from one side to another, trying to register the news and process the information. Soon, it seemed she came to terms with it because her eyes became standard size, and she wore an encouraging smile.

That was followed by a nod from the lady as if giving her approval. Holding her drink and brown bag, she went on her way leaving behind an extremely relaxed and confident Jay who was beaming with joy.

Gina had been examining the body language of the lady and took mental notes on the pretext to keep this relationship cordial, especially in his absence.

"Done!" He came in with a wide smile and twinkle in his eyes. "Cee-Cee was at first a little somber, but once I told her I'm going only for a week-long vacation, she was pleased and wished me luck."

"Okay, so I get her name is Cee-Cee." She nodded with raised eyebrows and continued, "So how has she paid you for a lifetime? I think even PayPal does not have that option." Gina was still curious since the last time they had a conversation about it.

Jay stood straight, accentuating his six-foot height and sighed deeply before giving out a smile, which highlighted his dimples. "Gina! I owe Cee-Cee my current life!"

Gina was shocked, appalled to hear this and could not resist, "Care to explain?" in an acerbic tone.

Jay took a deep breath and said in a cautious tone, "She has helped me set up this café. It was my idea, but she backed me emotionally and partially with finances."

Gina was filled with gratitude upon hearing it, but she would not let go easily. "Then how come I did not meet her during my last visit?"

Jay frowned, trying to remember. "She must have been out of town or something, Gina."

"Okay. That's believable, but why is she dressed like that?"

"What about it?" he asked in a questionable tone while approaching the register.

"She is clothed from top to bottom. Way too much clothing, huh?"

Jay got busy with a customer, and as a result, the question was side-tracked making Gina believe she was some weirdo talking to herself.

*********

Morning came quickly, and Jay was soon loading his bags in the trunk with a chirpy Yogi, who was clueless. "Your cruise leaves at four o'clock this afternoon, so why are you leaving so soon?" Gina queried, rubbing her sleepy eyes.

"No, I will leave from work. I'm going there to set things up. Will see you there," he said in a very excited tone rushing from one room to the other. "Also, you needn't worry about the miscellaneous bills. I have paid them in advance, and it's only a week-long excursion."

"Yes, a week will go by in a blink. Go and enjoy," Gina encouraged him, pointing toward the front door. Then, after a pause, she asked in a cautionary tone, "Did you text your mom?"

He stopped in his tracks as if the earth had stopped moving. The strain exhibited by Jay made his forehead wrinkle and his lips twirl as if he were in pain due to exertion. Gina observed from a distance and had dual feelings for him. At first, there was compassion which made her want to let go of the topic, but then she reminded herself of her promise never to desert her aunt, who brought her up with so much love and affection despite a vacuum in her life. She was quick to change her mental state while awaiting a response from her cousin.

"Gina, you know when I think of her, all my past memories come alive. Why do you want me to go back?" he said with eyebrows arched and hands on his hips in a melancholic tone.

"What is her fault in what happened to you? She has suffered more because of your dad deserting her than you have. You are her only blood relative still alive, and you choose to look the other way. She is still grieving the loss of her only sister!" Gina did not hold back.

"Sure, I can understand. But, I will always associate both my parents as one. I will never be able to differentiate between them," he justified his answer and drove off. She, in return, just nodded her head in dismal while texting her aunt about his status.

# CHAPTER FIFTEEN

*"Unbeing dead isn't being alive."* — **E.E. Cummings**

Later in the day, Gina took the reins of the café while wishing Jay luck and promising to be in touch at least for the sake of his store, if nothing else. The duo left for their drive to Los Angeles. It had been ages since Jay had gone for a long drive, so after filling gas and checking the tire pressure of his ten-year-old car, he started his journey that was estimated to be around seven to eight hours according to Google Maps, but he intended to take breaks in between for his sanity and Yogi's sake.

The radio was off since his emotions were high when he started his drive south on US Highway 101. Traffic was bearable as he had started early allowing himself to maintain an average speed of seventy miles per hour.

Yogi was confused and kept looking out of the window for his usual destination, but all he got to see were fields, trees, and bare mountains. Disappointed, he would curl back on the passenger seat next to his master, half-hoping that the brakes would be applied soon, and he'd get to rest on his usual couch in his typical surroundings. Jay noticed his confusion and muttered, "We are going on a lo-ooo-ng trip!" But the words, 'long trip' were foreign to him as he had never been on one since he was adopted. So, he would now and then raise his head to eventually drop it next to his paws.

Time was ticking along with the number of miles covered by the car in a mechanical way, but things were not going smoothly for the driver. He felt a trickle from his eye onto his cheek. His eyes were heavy due to the fluid in them, and he had to make a couple of quick blinks to get them to focus. His subconscious mind made him go down memory lane of some random incidents with his once beloved fiancée, Sasha—their long drives, her constant chit-chat, and his input for every darn thing followed by laughter, fake anger, disagreements, and contemplation over various topics that ranged from personal to political.

"Jeez, life was good, but *she is my past, and I'm going to make my present. "* he muttered, quickly wiping that tear off his cheek. Yogi was smart to feel the vibes and raised himself to look at him while arching his head. Jay was brisk to command, "Sit down, Yogi. No licking now," he said with a stern look to which he whimpered at first and then curled back on the seat.

Jay turned on the radio to FM 101.3, which diverted his attention as he hummed along to the diverse artists and their respective songs. When he got an overdose of music, he yearned for human company. That made him switch to a news channel—AM 740—which broadcasts CBS news updates and weekly television programs of *Sixty Minutes* and *Face the Nation* along with additional features that included traffic, weather reports, sports updates, and *Bloomberg Money Watch* business reports. He felt good momentarily since an actual human voice was interacting given the excessive miles he had to drive.

Frequent stops for the bathroom, snacks, and gas were made until they arrived at the harbor. The aura in the air was full of adventure and enthusiasm as travelers around him were parking and walking toward the huge ship. The duo master and pet walked toward the cruise line when Yogi gave a big woof. "Yes, this will be our home for one week," Jay remarked, speaking to him with frequent nods and eye contact.

They checked in, and each of them got their tags that were tied to their wrist and paws, respectively. It was just like being remanded but to a luxury home. With Yogi instructed to be monitored twenty-four-seven since there will be other canines on board, they walked with his trolley bag and small, leashed dog in the other hand.

When they entered the main deck of the ship, Jay was amazed at the decor in the lobby. It had eight long, glittering chandeliers with the ceiling decorated with gold-leafed cornice moldings. The replicas of paintings by masters were spellbinding in addition to hand-laid mosaic tiles all around. The flooring was marble with a sparkling flower motif in every four tiles.

His eyes were wide with awe, but soon they became a normal size when a 'Can I help you?' sound was heard from a distance. He looked in that direction to see a Help Desk. Jay was quick to nod and walked toward it. His first reaction to the pretty blonde was, "This is awesome. I can't believe that I am actually on a ship," to which she was quick to nod since she had probably heard it umpteen times. She followed with a smile as she scanned his papers and handed him his room key. She also briefly pet Yogi before inquiring his name and then handed him his complimentary goodie bag, which included a nametag, food bowls, and toys. Then she pulled out the deck plan of the ship.

"All the passengers have to attend the mandatory safety briefing an hour before the ship leaves the harbor." She circled the muster station where all the passengers were supposed to meet for a safety drill. She gave him the sail and sign card, which needed to be handed to the captain during the safety briefing, and he would sign it after the briefing. Next, she highlighted the route to his room, followed by some dine-in areas for breakfast and lunch along with the formal dining area for dinners.

"Welcome aboard!" she said with a twinkle in her eyes and a smile that seemed to be worn for hours ever since the boarding had started.

"Hey, buddy! We are going to have so much fun!" Jay literally choked due to enthusiasm while walking toward his assigned room. After a stroll for a good ten minutes, he got a glimpse of the pools, the spa room, the gym, and the different cafés leading them to an array of numbered rooms. As he passed by, he tried finding the door that matched his key number 1035.

"Finally, here we are," he said with glee to which Yogi made sure to add his enthusiasm with a woof.

They opened the door to find the decor minimal yet cozy with white walls adorned simply with a picture frame of a sunset over the ocean and a queen- size bed along with a sofa bed for the dog. There was a television set and a cabinet for storage. The room had a small balcony that opened outdoors with a seating for two and high rails for protection. Adjacent to the dog bed was a door that led to the washroom consisting of a commode, bathing stall, and sink.

"Small, but not bad, huh?" He arched his eyebrows looking down at Yogi who was no longer on the leash.

Jay was quick to unpack and place two bowls for his pet near the cabinet pouring gourmet dog food especially given for pet travelers. He filled the second bowl with the water from the tap of the bathroom, and before he could place it next to the food bowl, he saw Yogi already digging into it.

"Hungry, buddy?"

Seeing him munch made his stomach growl. Shutting the door of the balcony, he commanded, "I'm going to go get some food for myself. You stay put," to which Yogi just arched his head a bit to listen and then got back to his bowl while Jay locked the door of the room behind him.

The walk to the café was filled with courteous smiles as he nodded to all walking to their respective rooms. There were plenty with canines, and he was happy to know that Yogi will have company. While he was enjoying a snack of coffee and some eats, his phone beeped, and the screen was blinking.

**Gina**: *Reached?*

He exclaimed at first and then it was followed by a nod muttering, "How could I forget?"

Wiping his greasy hands, he typed.

**Jay**: *Yes, checked in.*

He followed by inserting a smiley emoji and then pressed Send.

After a pause, he realized the date and then started typing another message.

**Jay**: *Tomorrow is Halloween. FYI, I normally don't believe in giving away treats for free.*

He put his phone down and continued to sip his beverage when his phone beeped again, making him frown.

**Gina**: *I shall make that decision in your absence. You just enjoy your vacation. BTW, extra expenses will be incurred by me, and will not go through your bank account.*

The message was followed by a wink emoji.

"Huh." He was startled at first, staring at the mobile screen with wide eyes and an open mouth.

"Excuse me!" A gentle voice broke his reverie.

"Huh?" He was forced to come out of his thoughts to look.

It was a young, bespectacled brunette girl with braces who was smiling widely, waiting for him to look at her. Jay was quick to shut his mouth, wet his lips, and make a quick gulp.

"Can I take this chair?" she requested.

"Ah, sure." He was quick to nod while eyeing her actions as she placed her disabled chihuahua on it.

After a light snack, the ship blew its horn, which was notification that it was time for the meeting on the lower deck. Jay walked in that direction with the help of the deck plan and was amazed at the number of people already standing for the briefing.

"Hello there!" said the captain of the ship. "Welcome to the CH Cruise where not just humans but even your canine is welcome aboard!" That was followed by a couple of woofs from the microphone to create the effect that evoked laughter amongst the humans.

"During these six nights and seven days that you will spend here, you will not only enjoy the different shows we have planned for you all on the ship but will also be touring the Pacific Ocean and get a view of the islands from a distance while getting a chance to soak your feet in the mud of two islands as indicated on your itinerary."

Everyone cheered.

"I know. Isn't it exciting? I also guarantee that you all will gain at least five pounds when you get off this ship next Sunday!"

The audience went quiet.

The captain became serious, and after laying his right fingers over his goatee, he said in an accommodating tone,

"But that's a good thing! You ought to indulge in the menu that has been planned just for you. It's time to lay back, relax, and soak the sun with the different cocktails and scrumptious menu items."

That was followed by many nods and frolic.

The crew and the captain cheered along, and after a quick pause, one of the crew members requested, "If you can please come ahead near the railing of the ship."

The first-timers to this ship were confused but just followed orders while wearing a frown. Jay was one of them.

"You see these red boats. These are rescue boats. We have not used them since this cruise line was unveiled. That would be five years to be precise. And our sailing expedition is known to do a dry dock every year." The captain announced in an assertive tone, "But we all ought to be prepared for the worst, while we continue to enjoy only the best. If there is any emergency, the microphone will beep a vacate notice. And all of you have to assemble here with your canines on leash or in your arms, and the crew members will help you get on these rescue boats."

There was a peculiar silence in the air. Jay could feel the tension as his nerves tightened around his forehead. He could see the captain's mouth moving, but there was no voice he could hear. Jay was trying hard to gulp, and he realized his mouth was too dry to build up saliva.

Just then, his heart thumped, and his ears started ringing. He shook his head from left to right to get rid of that feeling and noticed people around him cheering, either with their raised hands or with their glasses. That confused him. But soon, the background music started making sense.

"Jimmy Buffet! You continue to be the party rocker after so many years, huh,"he mumbled, tapping his feet. "Drink it up, this one is for you! It's been a lovely cruise," he warbled along with others while wearing a small smile.

Melodious music can turn any moment into action and imagination.

"Jeez, I hope I sing this song when I reach the harbor next week." He crossed his fingers while eyeing those red rescue boats. He continued tapping his feet to the classic music created by the strums of a guitar and drums in the background, lifting the lovely lyrics of this singer. Soon, two long blasts were heard, and everyone gathered on the upper deck waving in excitement. The ship was leaving its berth.

Jay cheered momentarily, then walked with steady but quick steps to his room. Yogi was tugged beneath the sheets due to the noise and gave a loud woof at his master when he opened the door. Evening was a pleasant affair for the duo. Jay was exploring different decks with Yogi in his arms. They would halt now and then at the dog play areas that were fenced where Yogi would mingle with the other canines.

It was a delight to see how the dog who would try to initiate play will slap the other canine's front legs down on the ground repeatedly, while the other would give a big silly open-mouthed grin. The dogs would act silly by giving off bouncy movements while voluntarily falling down and exposing their bellies and then take turns chasing each other. Jay was enjoying recording all this with a smile as a proud parent while all the owners of the other canines were trying to mingle. One of them was a girl who was holding onto her chihuahua and enjoying the show while her pet would woof occasionally.

"Hey there."

He frowned.

"We met at the café where I took the chair adjoining to your table," she reminded him in a candid tone. He was quick to acknowledge with a broad smile while pointing toward Yogi who was playing and growling.

"Meet Yogi," he said with joy.

"Boy, he looks aggressive." She did not hesitate to comment.

Jay was quick to defend him. "That's how dogs play. He is my best pal."

"MeetMaggi. She is my guardian angel and savior. Don't go by this special cart that assists her to walk. Two months ago, she was like the others in the pen with all four legs intact, but she lost her two while saving me!"

"May I?" he asked before petting her, and soon Maggi was drooling with affection over him.

Yogi sensed it from afar and gave out a woof. He was quick to jump off the pen to rush toward his master. Standing close to Jay, he sniffed Maggi as if trying to analyze her and her special cart before settling near his master's legs. *I guess all who breathe the same air, have the shade of compassion within them.*

"Oh, that's so cute!" she remarked, looking at Yogi's behavior. "By the way, I am Sheela. Hope to bump into you more often during this one-week cruise."

"Absolutely." They parted ways.

That evening the duo tucked in early having decided to wake up earlier in the morning to catch the sunrise from their balcony and then proceed toward the top deck for a brisk walk followed by a leisurely breakfast.

In the morning, Jay got hold of the day's newspaper that highlighted the plans for the evening.

"Halloween night," Jay remarked reading the headlines. "Let's go shop since we have a party to go to tonight."

Yogi arched his head and looked surprised.

They went to the Fun Shop, and Jay was confused at seeing so many costumes for canines and humans.

"Yogi, I'm so confused. What would you like to be?" he asked his pet who was in his arms.

"Just pick one, buddy," he commanded, putting him down on the floor while keeping the leash in his hand. Yogi wandered around until he found one costume and kept sniffing at it and even attempted to nibble at the wrapping.

"Atta boy!" Jay was amused. "You're so smart. What could I have asked from a canine, huh?" He gave out a snickering laughter.

He dropped the costumes off at their room and walked to the Lido Deck to find a suitable reclining chair facing the aft. Yogi's leash was attached to the chair while Jay lay down in a reclining position staring at the vast ocean and the ripples created by the ship as it moved ahead. He was amused that the wrinkles were soon evened out as if the ocean was clearing the past, and the ship moved ahead in knots. No grudges. No memories. The past was being embraced as is. The ocean pervaded the ripples. *Just as Susan repeats in every session—embrace your past and move on.* He shut his eyes with an entertained smile and hummed a note unknowingly. These lyrics, courtesy of Alex Glasgow, were hummed when he was a child, and his family was comprised of both his parents.

*Dance Ti' Thy Daddy*
*Come here, maw little Jacky,*
*Now aw've smok'd mi backy,*
*Let's hev a bit o' cracky,*
*Till the boat comes in.*

********

Back in the small town of Los Altos Hills, Gina had bought all the Halloween decorations for the café on Monday night after informing Jay about it. She wanted to keep her budget at a minimum, so she and Sam decorated it with pumpkins, candles, some silver branches and dry leaves. White cobwebs were hanging all around the café along with lots of orange and black balloons while she planned on dimming the lights to give a dreary effect.

She knew that Halloween was a big thing in the United States, and thanks to Sam's input, they had even planned a special menu for Tuesday. While stacking up lots of lollipops and candies for the children, she premade the snacks with Sam's help. The two sets of hands moved articulately as one pair kneaded the mini pizza dough while the other pair decorated it with pumpkin, cheese, and olives. Then, they proceeded to the next venture where one individual sliced the cheese while the other shaped the pretzels and the cheese to make broomsticks. Gina went on to bake the lemon cupcakes while Sam peeled bananas.

Long after the book club had dispersed, they continued to remain busy with preparations doing everything with zeal, lots of laughter, and discussing various topics. Gina was amazed at how much they had in common.

They opened up to each other within a few hours, and she was really looking forward to the remaining six days with him. In fact, there were moments when she wanted just the two of them to be running this café without her cousin's interruptions.

"Is the chocolate sauce ready?" he inquired bringing out the pile of peeled bananas from the freezer near the stove.

The duo dipped the bananas in the sauce while trying to decide on the prices for each of the menu items.

"Hey, how about we have a special night instead of the usual chess night?" Sam inquired, making Gina's eyes pop. "What do you have in mind?"

"A mask party?"

"Err... what to expect from this?" Gina inquired in a confused tone as she placed monster eyes on the bananas.

"Let me get the supplies from the craft store while you inform Azra about the change in plans. I am sure he will love it!" Sam winked at her while continuing to clean up.

Gina was unsure. "I'm not sure if Jay will agree since he might be losing his commission for the evening, and Jay always likes to keep them happy."

"We still charge the usual for the class. As a result, Azra gets his share of profit, although I doubt he will take it since he is not going to instruct that night. But for Jay's sake, let's keep it all the same. Just the supplies will be extra, and we will need to be reimbursed for them, and we can have a fun night."

Gina enjoyed the business deal, and even proposed to chip in for the supplies. It was a new venture for one night, and that brought Gina and Sam quite close as they realized the thrill they felt and the many goosebumps when they would bump into each other or their hands would accidently brush each other. With their eyes blinking rapidly and hearts fluttering, they would gasp for a breath from the excitement of that silly laughter just to catch the other's attention. It was all there, and neither of them had any problems with their attraction to each other. In fact, they were enjoying every bit of the showcasing of their emotions.

Tuesday morning, Gina was excited to open the store and see the look of disbelief on the faces of the high schoolers who came in for their usual beverages. They were taken by surprise by the decor, the free candies, and even the snacks that marked the spirit of the holiday. The masked lady when she peeked into the brown bag also had a look of astonishment on her face and disappeared from the scene.

Evening came early especially since Gina was waiting with bated breath. The duo had arranged the supplies for the mask-making event. Azra was cool about it, leaving no grudges behind, and thankfully with Jay's ship cruising in the Pacific, there was no connectivity with him. Things were going just as planned, and Gina could not stop giggling over everything.

Evening brought in a lot of Trick-or-Treaters who had previously passed by this café labeling the owner as a 'sulky old man.' However, after peeking into the dreary old café, which usually is a well-lit one, they saw that celebrations were in full swing. Cheery children were coming in for the treats, and a mask-making session was in progress. The special menu was being purchased at a rate even quicker than the speed of a cheetah.

The clinking of the register, the immodest and friendly laughter along with the occasional boos were the stars of attraction. In a blink, the evening came to an end, and when the duo was finished cleaning up, they were counting their profits. Gina could not help but give out a loud exclamation which was followed by a small peck on Sam's cheek. Unknowingly, that moment came to haunt her within a few seconds when Sam stood still with a gleam in his eyes and a mouth wide open. She was embarrassed at first, then gently wiped her lipstick off his cheek with a tissue apologizing for the kiss.

"Don't be!" he said with a smirk, which she avoided to comment on and got back to her business.

********

Jay was stationed at that reclining chair until sunset when he thought of Gina, his café, and Cee-Cee. Soon the duo got up to get dressed for their first special night.

Jay went back to his room, and he did not hesitate to take many selfies with his phone. This was his first Halloween with his pet, and he wished to send their pictures across to his cousin, but given the cost of the Wi-Fi on the ship, he chose not to do that until they reach an island. They walked with pride toward the assigned dining room and did not hesitate to stop when professional photographers would ask them to pose in their costume.

"Yummy. You two make delicious sausages, I just want to eat you," was a comment that made Jay blush.

The party was comprised of all the masters being seated with their respective pets as they mingled and dined together with occasional woofs from some irritable canines that were getting restless in their master's arms. Canines and their humans were enjoying champagne toasts and doggie hors d'oeuvres provided by the special dining dog café. Soon the duo retired to their room while Yogi was happy to be free from that costume and be his naked self, tossing and turning on his sofa bed, but not for long!

# CHAPTER SIXTEEN

*"Life can only be understood backwards; but it must be lived forwards."* — **Soren Kierkegaard**

The ship was rocking due to the full waves, making Jay toss now and then. Yogi too would give out a silent woof. Finally, the master called his pet to his bed so that they could snuggle like old times, especially when Jay used to have nightmares. They both had had a fulfilling day. Soaking in the sun and touring the ship had taken a toll on them, but the evening was full of excitement as they both had ventured into something new for the first time. Their nerves were still taking time to relax while their bodes were tired, and now the ship was rocking back and forth. They both tossed and turned. Finally, when sleep still evaded them, Jay turned on the television to divert their attention.

He chose to watch the re-run of *Friends* where Joey, Phoebe, Rachel, and Ross try to get into the apartment for a Thanksgiving feast but has been locked from the inside by Monica and Chandler. The smell of food makes their tummies rumble. Monica tries to open the door with her duplicate key, but Chandler is quick to put on the monkey-door lock allowing the four to stick their heads in and stare at the food. Jay chuckled over their expressions and suddenly heard his stomach grumble in hunger.

He was craving a midnight snack. He checked the newsletter to find if any cafés were open during that hour, and a paper slid underneath the door. It was a leaflet with a picture of a young man named Dan. He was an on-board kennel master who would assist dog owners while they were on the ship. He would help with the regular feedings, walks, indoor playtime, and clean up. Jay was impressed and showed the picture to Yogi who sniffed the picture to give out a gentle woof. Jay patted him gently, "We will meet Dan tomorrow," and went back to browsing for cafés open at this late hour.

Putting Yogi's leash on, he walked toward a café while being cautious of his steps as the ship continued to rock now and then due to the turbulent ocean. As he approached to climb the stairs, he saw a 'closed' sign. Perplexed, he inquired of a staff member who was observing him. "The map indicates that the café above would be open at this hour. Why is this closed sign preventing me to walk up to the lido deck?"

"Sir, the weather has changed for the worst. To keep you all safe, we had to shut down the deck. However, the midship is open for eats." He grabbed his deck plan and circled it.

"Weather changed?" Jay was quick to gulp. "I am hoping it is just temporary."

"I'm sure, sir. Once the sun is out tomorrow morning, the waves will settle in. Today being a full moon night... we could blame that for now," he said with a confident smile that made Jay quickly agree as he walked toward the circled late-dining café. He was surprised to see many people hanging around the café, and what was even more amazing was that they were all talking as if they had known each other for ages.

Once he ordered, he grabbed a chair. He tried to lend a patient ear at first, and then was quick to nod giving out a crooked smile.

"Adversity brings people together," he mumbled.

The rocking ship concerned many who had chosen to hang around with like-minded people to discuss their options or just to relax. Soon Jay was also showcasing his opinion, and there were some who agreed to his theory. Time was ticking away as the clock stuck midnight, but no one was concerned they were vacationing on this cruise. The leashed canines sniffed each other for a while and then retired until their masters unleashed and carried them to their respective rooms.

Morning came late for Jay even though Yogi kept licking him. They both strolled along the promenade deck and then settled on the lido deck for a hearty breakfast. Jay had no interest to browse through the itinerary for the day. He just wanted to meet Dan. Once the duo was finished with breakfast, they headed to the assigned deck to meet the young man who would be his pet's caretaker when needed.

"Dan?" Jay inquired in a restrained tone.

The young man was quick to get up from a kennel and look toward the voice, "Yes."

Jay handed him the leaflet before introducing Yogi who was in his arms.

"Hey there, buddy!" Dan stroked Yogi's fur with his long palm. "May I?" he asked Jay who looked at his pet for a signal and once he realized how comfortable Yogi was, he handed him slowly to Dan. There were a couple of woofs at a distance to which Dan nodded his square face with minimum hair, showing his ears that poked out like a leprechaun. His tanned olive skin was flawless and clean-shaven as he walked toward them with steady steps. Jay felt as if he were speaking their language since all the canines after a couple of sniffs and grunts were soon obeying his orders as if he had cast a spell over them.

"Would you like to take a break? Maybe a stroll around the ship or whatever suits you," Dan inquired. "Today, I will be taking them to the doggie pool where they will swim."

"Do you think it's good weather to swim?" was Jay's first reaction. "I mean look at the fog out there. I can hardly keep warm in this cotton jacket of mine," he clarified.

Dan gave an amused smile. "I understand your concern, sir. But first, the water is warm, and second, canines can handle this kind of cold temperature."

Jay was quick to change the conversation once convinced.

"Wow, Yogi loves swimming," Jay said with glee. "I, on the other hand, am scared of water, so I have never ventured out with him. Can I watch you?"

"Sure. That is if you have no place to go to." Dan smiled.

With the help of an assistant, the duo was putting diapers on the dogs. It was a chaotic situation as some would try to walk in circles to avoid putting their other foot through while there were some canines that wore them without any resistance but now wanted to break free. They would either keep moving around hoping the diaper would fall off or were attempting to tear it apart.

Jay was amused by the whole affair and did not hesitate in taking videos.

"Hi there, sorry I am late." A voice made Jay quickly turn his head since it sounded familiar.

"Sheela."

"Hi. I will be there in just a minute." After helping Maggi with her diaper, she settled her with Dan.

"Yogi seems excited," she remarked, sitting next to Jay.

"Aha! He loves swimming, but because of me, he never got to explore a pool. I would just make him waddle in the bathtub." He laughed. "But the sight here is just beyond hilarious." He shared some videos with her, making her chuckle.

Soon Dan was in the doggie pool with the leashes holding the canines as they all wiggled and squirmed trying to adjust to the temperature of the pool. Dan was muttering something to them. Jay noticed he wore a belt which had all the leashes attached, leaving his hands free. Soon he stepped into the five-foot pool and would occasionally pet some dogs if they needed attention.

It took a good ten minutes for all of them to settle in. Then the assistant jumped in with Maggi without her wheels. And in no time at all, the canines were waddling around the pool splashing water all over with human laughter echoing in the background. Eventually, other dog owners joined in as it was getting close to their pool time.

Jay was happy to share those videos of the canines, which helped him forge a bond as it touched a special chord in their hearts. Thanks to Dan, Jay and Yogi found new friends. The canines were starving after their exercise, and the dog keeper treated them to special dog hors d'oeuvres, even offering to keep them in his quarters for their naps while their owners chose to mingle with each other.

The golden sun seemed to say goodbye while setting down for the day, and Jay, along with his new friends—Sheela, John, Ethan, William, and Mia—chose to dine together in a formal gathering donning their best attire while their pets enjoyed their cuisine with fun and play in a dog-friendly environment.

The highlight of the evening was the number of pictures they took. Solo selfies, selfies with each other while dining, and then selfies with their pets, their phones were flooded with a plethora of group pictures. They called it a night with their laughter still ringing in their minds. The ocean was behaving well tonight in spite of the fog. But, alas, not for long.

# CHAPTER SEVENTEEN

*"This is your life and it's ending one moment at a time."* — **Chuck Palahniuk**

A loud fog horn blew and was followed by a couple of bursts. That led to chaos on the ship since all the canines got the fright of their lives and began to bark in unison. The horn was so loud and sudden that even the humans took a while to get a grip.

*Bang!*

That gave a jolt to the ship. All the dogs stopped barking for a microsecond, and then they followed suit as if they were doing a counter attack on their opponent, although they were clueless who their enemy was. Humans, on the other hand, were still absorbing the shock. However, their intellect made them aware that something was terribly wrong, but they needed a sign from their captain before they jumped to any conclusions.

An announcement was made to stay in your rooms. However, people with balconies chose to stand there to satisfy their curiosity about the loud bang and the fog horn. The actions around the ship made Jay's heartbeat flutter. He blinked his eyes rapidly as he tried his best to look through the dense fog enveloping them while his hand was constantly on his pet trying to pacify him.

Jay could scarcely see a couple of emergency boats in the ocean with a few heads in them. The number of flashlights illumining on each of the two boats made him identify the number of people in each of them. Their white uniforms were illumined thanks to the beacon. They were seen rowing toward the front of the ship. When they passed under his balcony, Jay wished he could listen to their conversations with voices that were strained and heavy with emotion. Soon they disappeared as if the dense fog ate them. Their voices were now muffled.

Totally oblivious to the cool temperature, he waited for them to row back. His heart continued to beat fast in fear and anticipation of his worst fears coming true. Yogi could sense the feeling and would keep licking him at regular intervals. Time was ticking, and it felt like an eternity for him since the people in the rowboats seemed to be taking their own sweet time.

Soon the boats were rowing back, and this time with lots of energy with the crew talking continuously to each other in a tone that was rushed and inattentive. He did not like the energy that was being thrown around. He gulped many times while he strained hard to make sense of what was happening. Just then, he heard a knock. Jay was quick to place Yogi on the bed and approached the door.

"Hello, sir. We have an emergency and need to vacate the ship. Please carry your pet and any medications that you need, and walk toward the muster station where we had our briefing on the first day of embarkation. For your information, here is the way to get to it." A crew member in uniform had a deck map where the station was circled and the route highlighted.

"What happened?" Jay inquired with knitted eyebrows and a scratchy throat.

"We have had a collision with a rock due to the dense fog, and there is a big crack in the bow of the ship."

Jay wanted to ask more, but the uniformed guy walked ahead.

"But... but—"

"Sir, please follow directions and come down to the muster station."

Jay quickly shut the door. He looked around with starry eyes to which Yogi gave out a woof. Jay was quite preoccupied to respond to it. He could not concentrate for a bit, so he sat down on the edge of the bed to gather his thoughts. After a few seconds, he quickly got dressed, collected all his cash, his credit card from the safe, phone, covered his pet with the blanket, and started to walk toward the assigned meeting place.

Yogi could sense the crisis and wanted his master to utter those few words, 'It's gonna be okay,' but unfortunately, Jay was unsure of their future, so he just kept walking, holding his pet tightly in his arms. He met many people along the way who were as worried and tense as him. They all would exchange a note or two while walking with steady steps and holding their pets close.

Soon, after a good ten-minute walk which seemed like an eternity, they reached the station where life jackets and flashlights were being handed out. Jay was quick to make Yogi wear one while he wore the other over his jacket. He placed his wallet and essential goods in his inner jacket pocket that was zipped while holding the flashlight tightly. He was standing there for further directions until a crew member held his shoulder and directed him to an emergency boat. "Sir, please climb on that boat, and then we will lower it."

Jay gave a nervous gulp looking at Yogi with moist eyes, and the duo walked toward the assigned boat. He gently placed his pet, and was preparing to seat himself when he heard a distressed voice, "Please, somebody, please stop it."

He looked around since the voice, even though distressed, sounded familiar. It was Sheela requesting people to stop the wheels of Maggi's cart that had come off while she was loading her on the boat nearby. Jay saw that set of wheels pass by him. He was quick to bend and grab them, but they got kicked away by a fellow passenger who was just as nervous. Jay followed it. He was so determined to get those wheels that he missed out on the woof of his pet. He also missed out on the announcement of the crew member, "Sir, please sit. This boat is going to be lowered next."

He was just a man on a mission. His mission was those pair of wheels as if getting hold of that cart will get him out of this adversity to a happily ever after. All he wanted was a vacation with his pet. Nothing more and nothing less.

"Wait, Yogi." He looked back. "Yogi," he shouted, but the boat was being lowered so he could not see him. All he could hear was his constant woofs. Just then, there was a tap on his shoulder, "Sir, is this yours?" A passenger handed him the wheels.

He stared at them and looked toward Sheela, who seemed to be standing on the other side of the ship given the number of people in between them. He lurched with the set of wheels dodging people while announcing with a high pitch, "Coming through. Excuse me." He even brushed off a handful of shoulders in his way without any inhibitions until he reached her. She was holding Maggi in her arms and was quick to peck Jay on his cheek for the efforts. He blushed for a bit, forgetting that all this evacuation was just a dream until someone pushed past him and brought him back to reality. He heard his Yogi's woof, and his eyes widened as he ran toward his rescue boat.

The crew man standing next to it shouted in a restrained tone, "Sir, careful! You can board the other rescue boat. This one is not safe to board since it has lowered significantly."

Jay did not pay heed to his words. He jumped from the deck aiming toward the boat. There were four other passengers in the boat along with Yogi who were shouting, "Be careful."

While Jay's eyes were locked on his pet and the space in between where he was supposed to land, just then Yogi moved to that space where Jay was about to land. With his one foot already in the boat he tried to move the other foot away that was in the air so he wouldn't hurt his pet while landing, and that's when he tripped, and the passengers of the boat exclaimed in horror, "Oh my God."

Jay could not balance himself and flipped over. Sliding past his pet, he fell with a splash into the ocean. That impact made everybody quiet as they had not anticipated this. After assessing the scene, the white uniformed crew was quick to shout out, "Look out! Hold on! We're getting help!" as they communicated on their walkie-talkies trying to come up with a plan to rescue Jay. While this was happening, the passengers around stood still, trying to digest what had just happened. For those few minutes, they forgot they were given orders to evacuate the ship. They drew a blank on why they were even there because all they could perceive at that moment was a human falling in the big ocean. Jay had no control and was panicking. The bystanders could do little but feel helpless even though they were hundreds in number, but compared to the chilling turbulent water in the dark skies, they were nothing.

Yogi, on the other hand, had increased the decibel of his barking and moved around restlessly. At first, the passengers in that boat held onto him. But they could not hold him for long as he slid away from the hands that were holding on to him. The transition from being on a vacation to having to abandon their holiday space abruptly in the middle of the night was not easy to accept. The hands let go, and the pet was quick to jump in the cold water, especially since he was aware of his master's fear of water. Yogi did not have the intellect to reason out on how to help, but he sure had his heart in the right place. Canines are known for compassion, and he proved he was true to his class. So, be it!

Now the master and the pet were in the ocean while flashlights were shining over them with loud suggestions, essential recommendations, powerful assertions, and heartfelt sympathies. The scene was utterly chaotic. Even though the crew members wanted to suggest something, they were not able to get it across to Jay. The mayhem that had ensued left Jay feeling utterly lonely and desperate even though so many people surrounded him. From the moment he splashed in the chilling ocean, he was having various thoughts.

*Darn holiday! I am not destined to have one! Why did I come?*

*Why did I crave for something that is not for me? Hasn't life already taught me enough! Damn foolish of me! I am going to die in this ocean!*

*I wish I had said goodbye to mom.*

Just then, he got a flashback of his reoccurring nightmares. The drowning and a voice calling out to him," You can do it! Don't give up! Not yet! I need you!"

All of a sudden, his eyes widened as he recognized the voice that was his silent inspiration all these years.

"Mom!" he said out loud. *Oh God! How could I have not recognized that voice! Oh no! I can't die. Who will take care of her? I can't desert her like dad did!*

Jay, being scared of water, was splashing his arms violently while straining to keep his face above water. And his legs were kicking hard under the water scared that a shark would come and get him from underneath. Yogi was waddling with steady and confident strokes toward him more so since the water was his comfort zone. Although there were moments when Yogi would just pause and look confused as Jay would keep changing directions due to his nervousness, making Yogi tired and confused.

The captain of the ship was busy giving an S.O.S. signal while the crew members threw an inflatable three-seater boat into the ocean, announcing it to Jay. Given how jumpy and spooked he already was, their voices fell on deaf ears.

However, once the boat was in the water, the passengers in the rescue boat using their paddles were pushing it toward the dog. At first, Yogi got scared and barked loudly at it. It took a while for him to adjust to it since he thought it was an intruder, but then he heard a familiar command by someone in the rescue boat, who was pushing it toward him.

"Climb," he commanded while Yogi tried to obey him, but he made quite a few fumbles since the boat would slip or slide away or topple when he would try to follow the command.

Finally, he climbed into the inflatable boat and stayed but was very nervous as the boat was moving. Yogi showed his nervousness by barking, but the passenger in the rescue boat gave a stern command, "Stay."

He looked at him with curiosity and then sat down with his head between his paws. Jay was huffing and puffing. Initially, he would shout "Help," "Yogi," or "Save me" occasionally, but now even those words were not coming out since the chilly water was draining him as his body was trembling because of his fear and the unfriendly ocean. He lay on his back, and thanks to the life jacket, stayed afloat with not much motion or activity. This helped the passengers on the rescue boat come to action. While two sets of hands were rowing their boat, another set of hands was pushing the inflatable boat toward Jay while Yogi sat still.

Jay's eyes were closed as he continued to murmur. Neither did he care about those thousands of eyes glued to him, nor was he interested in the hundreds of flashlights on him. He was in his own world of fear, anger, and cynicism. With his eyes mostly shut to avoid the salty water, he was cursing himself recollecting all the incidents with his mom as a kid, a teen, and as an adult.

Minutes had turned into hours, and with the water gushing into the damaged ship, there was not much time to waste. Although the captain had sent out the stress signal, the crew members got busy unloading the rest of the passengers only after noticing a couple of red rescue boats paddling and making efforts to rescue Jay in the water. The dog lay on the boat with the 'stay' command as he needed every now and then a 'good dog' compliment from the passenger who had commanded him in the first place.

The cold, crisp water made Jay unconscious, and when the collapsible boat reached him, Yogi got the scent of his master and gave out a loud woof. No reaction. He woofed around for help, especially toward the human who would command him but realized everyone was in their respective boats, so with his teeth, he pulled his master onboard. Dragging him on the boat partially by clutching on his jacket, he paused for a bit to take a breather, but that 'bit' led to the inflatable losing its balance as it capsized. Now both were in the water.

That sudden action gave a jerk to his master, who was quick to wake up with a gasp. With back and forth attempts to climb, they finally got on board. The rescue boats around cheered with loud claps as if they had seen land. But to see their travel mate safe was more than a win or success.

# CHAPTER EIGHTEEN

*"Live to the point of tears."* — **Albert Camus**

Now all the passengers were in their respective boats trying to make sense of what was happening. They all made sure to row the boats in the direction shown by their captain. The big ocean seemed like a white sheet that was stretched out far and wide with no land in sight. The red boats seemed as if they all were having a fun night on the wide ocean, but given the dark skies, the fog, and the cold temperature, it did not seem like a picnic at all. There would be instances when a handful of passengers would break down wailing or cursing. To boost everyone's spirits, the captain would now and then speak in the microphone giving the latest news—a ship is close by or how are you all doing?

But every minute seemed eons, and the passengers seemed to age due to the anxiety they were feeling like there was no tomorrow. They were growing restless since they were still stunned over the sudden turn of events. Keeping fingers and legs crossed, they could just try to stay warm, taking turns to be on watch-out while the others tried to snooze.

Just then, a huge wave startled everybody. The tides started shaping up in the ocean. It lifted their boats, making the passengers and their canines howl in panic. The ocean was echoing with their outbursts. Despite it all, the captain continued giving out instructions on how to paddle their boats. While everyone was keeping their boats at bay, Jay and Yogi's collapsible was not doing so well. It was drifting off at a much speedier rate than the others, and with Jay being unconscious most of the time, he was not aware of his surroundings. He would pat his pet now and then, just to make sure he was there and drift off again. For him, his universe was small—it consisted of his pet and since he was close by, he had no worries as long as they were in motion. Yogi had the company of his master, so he snuggled next to him.

The time when all the attention was on the collapsible boat and Yogi and his master, was long forgotten. Since people in their respective boats had their minds full with thoughts for their safety, they were only following the captain's orders. Soon, the rays of the sun were visible, and they all heaved a small sigh of relief. Firstly, they would be able to see clearly since the fog would take a back seat, and secondly, it would give warmth to their bodies while also giving them a ray of hope.

"Hang in there, the rescue ship is just a few knots away," was the announcement from the captain trying to put jelly over the charred toast that had been buttered thanks to the sunrise. That announcement made everyone taste that sweet jelly as they wet their lips and listened to their growling stomachs. They all were banking on him and the rescue mission that was chartered by the captain and his crew members. The intensity of the sun had increased making all the passengers a little irate, but soon a fog horn was heard in the distance, and that made all the passengers express their joy out loud.

Some passengers expressed it as if they had won a billion-dollar lottery. While a few wailed loudly as they now got a second chance for life promising themselves to be more mindful, a handful of passengers had their hands conjoined as they thanked the Lord while crying uncontrollably. However, most gave out a jubilant shout. The canines were confused seeing the reaction as they did not have the mental ability to understand whether it was a verbalization for worry or celebration. They gave out loud woofs until their masters consoled them with repeated pats.

Yogi and Jay were so far apart from the others that the fog horn sounded like a loud burp to them as if one of the animals in the ocean had just digested their food. It did surprise Yogi, but when he checked the surroundings, they seemed peaceful with no ripples in the ocean, so he felt at ease. While the master was in his own world still coming to terms with what destiny made him experience, with the sun above the horizon, Jay was suffering from a bad headache and kept wailing about it with his eyes still shut. Yogi was getting desperate hearing his moaning and would sometimes lick him, trying to splash some water over his face or at times even woof. Although the canine was curious where the other boats had gone, he would bark in all the four directions, but Jay could not understand it. Unfortunately, both Jay and Yogi were speaking a different language and had no common ground to relate.

# CHAPTER NINETEEN

*"If you don't know where you're going, any road will take you there."* — **George Harrison**

The ship rescued the red boats. All passengers were relieved to be away from the cold, barren environment and get that back-to-home feeling. As they climbed to the deck, they were welcomed with a blanket that was thrown around each one of them, which not only gave them warmth but also comfort that they were in safe hands and away from the wide-brimmed landscape that only exhibited the color blue. It was an eerie feeling to be with Mother Nature at its rawest, especially since they were forced to evacuate a ship they had the intention of calling it their home away from home for one week, hoping to unwind from the daily humdrum.

Little did any of them know that the weather would cast a spell over this ship, and it would get knocked over by a rock making them all spend a night under a hardly visible star-studded sky, thanks to the dense fog. Thereafter, they were exposed to the blaring sun that clanged its rays through the fog right into their skin making them wonder where the darn ozone layer had disappeared to.

While waiting for the rescue ship, the passengers were noticing how water was gradually filling up the giant ship and steadily pervading over it. Soon the big ship sank with a ghastly noise. All the passengers and their canines were left dumbstruck. The passengers were pondering over the little memories they had formed in those forty-eight hours and their personal items that most of them had shopped for especially for this trip were 'going down the drain' thanks to the wreckage!

The canines were curious about the horrifying sound, and could not react given the stark silence from their masters. Once on the deck away from the direct water and in the warmth of concerned people, the captain gave out a peppy speech. But no passenger was in the mood to cheer along. Now, their next mission was to get home where they could rest their bones in its warmth. But the captain did not want to leave them so easily. He wanted to brag of no casualty in spite of the evacuation in the middle of the night that not only consisted of humans but canines. He felt heroic and praised his entire crew.

Amidst all the drama, Sheela, along with Maggi in her arms, was moving around her fellow passengers with a keen eye. Her eyes were looking for someone, but not being able to find him or his pet, she grew restless and could not resist shouting out his name. "Jay!" She announced his name a couple of times looking in various directions with no response. That created stillness in the air as the passengers became anxious. Many passengers got up and repeated the name by walking further in and out just in case this individual had tucked himself in one corner of the ship trying to get comfort within, but no response.

That alarmed the captain and the crew members. They gulped, while the captain was quick to throw his shawl to one side and frantically search for something in a bag. Soon, he pulled out a bunch of papers.

"Okay, I will be taking your attendance. Please 'aye' me once I call out your name," he said in the microphone, wiping a trickle of sweat on his forehead with the back of his hand. Taking a deep breath, he silently sent a prayer upward for all the names on his roster to be present and soon, he started calling out names.

"Aye."

"Aye."

"Aye."

It was a delight to hear those yes's as another crew member took note of it. But not for long!

"Jay Sethi."

No response!

He gulped and repeated his name with a higher decibel, but no reaction from the audience. All the passengers looked around hopelessly. Some passengers hoped this person must have snoozed and asked the captain to speak louder. The captain repeated and repeated until his voice choked. He was quick to hide his emotions by assuring that the person must be around and went to complete the remaining names on the list.

Once done, the captain and crew were making notes when Sheela did not care before interrupting. "He is the person on the collapsible boat. Maybe he drifted off. We should S.O.S. the nearby islands," she suggested.

"That's exactly what we were supposed to do. Thank you for your concern and tip." He smiled graciously with a gentle tap on her pet.

"We should try to find him soon," she continued in a tender tone. "He is scared of water, but is a wonderful man."

"Yes! Absolutely! Every passenger is important to me," said the captain as he stepped aside to discuss some matters with the other crew members

She continued to stand there, and with moist eyes, she spoke in the microphone, "He is the guy who fell in the water and was alone in the collapsible boat." She choked while speaking. Most of them nodded their heads in dismay while some put their hands over their mouth to express their disappointment. The sea, when they were vacating the ship, was their playground. All had assembled there and were fighting in their own way to keep themselves alive. However, the advantage for all was they were in a group in one red boat. They all were different bodies but breathing in unison when any calamity would strike, while Jay was alone with his faithful dog that had swam to him when his master was in distress. Now both were missing. The passengers had a certain guilt feeling within as it could be observed in the silence that came after Sheela's announcement. Then, finally, some people spoke.

"The fog ate him up," came one opinion.

"The sharks!" someone else said with wide eyes and sweat forming on his forehead.

"Maybe another boat rescued him."

"He must have landed on some island. Let the captain check all the coordinates nearby."

With so many people giving their precious two cents, the captain who at first was nodding, had to excuse himself, leaving Sheela in anguish. The search started high and low with lots of messaging here and there, but no luck! The captain with a heavy heart made his announcement and ordered the ship to start sailing to its destination.

The mood was somber on the ship. To lose two lives even though they did not mean anything to them was heartbreaking. People whose lives he had touched in that short span of time were just a number on the ship. The passengers did not refrain from listening to the stories and incidents that Sheela and a handful of others related when they had dined with him and Dan had taken care of their pets.

# CHAPTER TWENTY

*"It is said that your life flashes before your eyes just before you die. That is true, it's called Life." —* **Terry Pratchett**

Back home, things were going smoothly. It had been only three days since Jay had left, but it seemed like an eternity for Gina. The waking early was the toughest part of her job while the rest went along in stride.

The business continued to boom. It sure was a lot of hard work from her end—early mornings and late nights—but the smiles and the tips had multiplied, and that made it all worthwhile. Gina was consistent in keeping a tab on the accounts while also enjoying the company of Sam, whose friendship was getting stronger each passing day. The at-first girly chuckles had become mature talking and actually led to conversations that made them know each other's likes and dislikes. When the clock would sound off its blaring alarm, she would toss and turn and moan, but then as her mind would fast forward the day for her—Sam, his smile, and the interesting conversations—it would make her actually get out from her cozy comforter and warm bed.

She was also thrilled that the lady dressed like a mummy from top to bottom for her scheduled pick-up of drink and snack would occasionally inquire about her welfare and even smile. She was ecstatic when she did the first time and did not hesitate to express her delight to her evening partner, who was quite impressed with her tactics. Along with holding down the fort for her cousin, she also continued her research and was astonished upon hearing the feedback from Jay's regulars.

"I like him, but he is a miser."

"He takes care of my orders, but then he loves money."

"He has a motive for everything."

"He means well, but I wish he would loosen up a little."

"I love his beverages. He is an honest person but very calculative."

Some of those assessments upset her. She remembered vividly how he would always be on her side when she moved in with his family and shared everything that he owned. He had no apprehension or attachment to any of his favorite toys, cars, or Legos that he spent hours making. If broken, he would let go of them easily.

"Damn the circumstances, thanks to Sasha! It has made him cling to his stuff for comfort," cursed Gina cleaning up one weeknight.

Just then, her phone buzzed. It was from some number starting with 1-800, and thinking it to be a spam caller, she avoided it. After locking up the store and saying adios to Sam, she settled in her car and glanced at her blinking screen.

'Huh, voice mail?'

The curiosity soon turned into a frown, since she could not believe what she heard the first time. With trembling fingers, she played it again and again with moist eyes. Pausing for a bit to digest the fact, she then called the number.

"Ms. Mehra?" asked the lady at the other end.

"Yes. This is Ms. Mehra speaking."

"Hi. You were listed as an emergency contact for Jay Sethi."

"Yes... yes. What happened to him?" she asked in a shaky voice while trying to keep her tears in check.

"Did you hear about the cruise? It was wrecked, and the passengers had to evacuate."

"Oh my God! I do not keep a tab on the news. But is my cousin safe?" she asked in a rushed tone while keeping her heart rate in check.

"Err... he is missing, but the crew is actively looking for him. This is the first incident for this cruise, and they will not let it pass easily." The lady on the other end of the phone tried to assure her in an optimistic tone by explaining various actions the crew planned on taking, but nothing seemed to pacify Gina.

Gina's legs were shaking restlessly, and she chose to get out of her SUV and walk while listening to the lady's thoughts.

Sam happened to drive by after having stopped at a nearby McDonald's for takeout. He glanced and was taken aback to see Gina wandering around the car. He pulled up near the café, paused for a bit, and then got out of his vehicle to study her body language.

She did not pay heed to him as she was pounding the paved street with her every step as if cursing over darn destiny! Her breath was unsteady. One hand was twirling her hair, and the other had the phone stabbed to her ear as if it would penetrate within.

Seeing all this made his heart flutter. He took a couple of deep breaths and then walked toward her. The moment she saw him, she fled to him and hugged him while still keeping the phone tugged to her ear. She cried loudly with no barriers. He was confused but continued to hug her and be patient. Finally, when she got a breather, she let loose and hung up the phone with the promise that the lady will keep her updated.

"Jay has gone missing," she declared, wiping her tears.

"What?"

"Yes, you heard me right. He and Yogi have gone missing. The ship wrecked, and they floated away. I pray the big ugly ocean has not swallowed them." She could not control herself and bawled.

Sam was quite overwhelmed himself to pacify her. He just stood there with a frown and looking very confused. It took him a while to ground himself, and then his hand reached out to Gina, but he could not come up with words of consolation.

It was a November evening when the winds had started blowing, dipping the temperature considerably. But circumstances had made their bodies insensitive to the cold as they stood there unperturbed by the fury of Mother Nature—this incident had shaken and stirred them up like a James Bond's martini.

"Life is not fair," Gina mumbled, fidgeting with her phone. "All he wanted was a holiday after all this time. Look, what he has got himself into." She continued to wipe her tears that were flowing nonstop. "What will I tell his mom? My grandparents won't be able to bear another loss."

"They will find him. It has never happened before. This cruise line is very promising. They have to find him for their company's sake," he said with a shaky tone.

While she nodded with the hope he is proven correct, Sam was trying to get the logistics straight, so he inquired further on his smartphone and was shocked to read about the cruise accident. The duo chose to hang around together, eventually having a bite or two for dinner. The night was not good for Gina as she kept contemplating informing his mom. This time the alarm clock buzzed, but she was awake before that. Gina grinned at the droning sound that she used to love to hate, but not today since fate was playing games with her.

The following day was a drag for her. She was wearing a fake smile with her phone held tightly with one hand even though at times the chores needed two. She kept holding on to it as if clinching it will get her cousin back. At the sunset hour, she had moist eyes since it was not only rewinding the day when she got the news of her parents' demise but also the moments when her cousin became her brother. He had hugged her lovingly and shared the little toys that were precious to him. She reminisced all those moments when he stuck with her at school, forming a shield when there would be moments of teasing and mocking with regards to her behavior and physical stature.

She lost track of time amidst all those memories until the lady dressed like a mummy tapped on the window of the café. That particular knock, the vibration felt on the glass that was adjacent to where she was standing, was enough to break her reverie. She quickly wiped her tears and got back in the store rousing to be professional like her cousin. Sam had taken hold of the evening fort after his daytime job and was two steps ahead of her. He had the order ready and was quick to hand her the beverage along with the brown bag. Gina gave a smile filled with gratitude and headed out.

"Hi." She heaved out a big sigh handing her the packet, but this lady felt the vibes and stood there staring at Gina's eyes.

Gina did not pay much attention to her, and after handing the stuff to her; she was about to turn around when something held her shoulder. She turned back, "Is something wrong?" she inquired with a frown. "Did I get your order wrong?" She instantly knew Sam might have gotten it mixed up, so she was quick to apologize.

"Something is wrong with you." This lady was blunt and came to the point.

Gina was shocked at her accurate analysis and gulped consciously loud enough to hear the saliva trickle down her throat.

"What do you mean?" she inquired in a passive tone.

"Heard from Jay?"

Gina bit her lower lip in contemplation.

"Is he okay?"

That's when Gina burst out crying.

She did not realize she still had it in her to cry more since she had shed maybe a gallon or three of tears in front of Sam and by herself in the apartment. The pain and agony were still hurting her, and she did not care about the bystanders seeing or hearing her. The lady's eyes were fixed on her as she wanted more information, and Gina wanted to get this off her chest since the phone had not rung since last night. "Look," she paused, "Cee-Cee..." then she glared into her eyes to get the confirmation that she got the name right.

But instead, this lady continued to stare at her with cold eyes that also meant *get to it!* Gina blinked a couple of times and then blurted out the facts. That shook the ground underneath Cee-Cee. The beverage spilled as she tried to find her composure. Gina was quick to hold her upper arm and noticed how frail she was. No flesh. She felt like just a stark humorous bone with no fat over it. Cee-Cee resisted, and Gina was quick to let go of her.

There was an awkward silence. Gina wiped her tears as her mind was thinking of Cee-Cee's bony structure and that big, wide layer of clothing she wore over it.

*What's up with this woman? Who is she?* Gina wondered.

Cee-Cee broke her trance.

"Yes, I will let you know as soon as I hear from the helpline." Gina forced a smile on her face before heading back to the café. "Will see you tomorrow."

She walked back with brisk steps and observed how Cee-Cee was walking gingerly and soon was out of sight. Sam interrupted her chain of thoughts, but she was not hesitant to say it out loud. "I want to follow this lady to see where she lives and what she does. Unfortunately, Jay has always kept her a mystery to me. I have to find out." She seemed determined.

Sam just chuckled over it and did not hesitate to comment, "Good for you. In fact, anything that can take your mind off Jay for now is good."

She raised her eyebrows and arched her head to show her displeasure. He pretended not to see it, and soon the duo got busy with the evening class. The show had to go on just as Jay would have wanted.

# CHAPTER TWENTY-ONE

*"Even death has a heart."* — **Markus Zusak**

Morning turned to noon, and the moaning continued. Soon it was time for the sun to say goodbye for the day. Luck was in their favor, and that's when the boat stopped abruptly. Jay was out cold. Yogi tried his best to revive him. No luck!

This canine looked at the surroundings where the inflatable washed ashore. He observed the sandy beaches and the coconut groves. Giving out a woof, he jumped on the shore and sniffed around following his nose that hinted at humans nearby making him bark loudly sending out a signal for help. He kept wandering around hoping to find somebody... anybody that inhaled the same air as them.

"Hey little doggy... where did you come from?" asked a voice that was tiny and sharp at the same time.

Yogi was at first taken aback, looking at a person who was chewing some mulch that came off a long white stick. Momentarily, he stepped back looking at that stick, then took a step forward. Sniffing at the stick and then sniffing at the person, he started to give out loud woofs in a way asking him to follow him and started running toward the shore. This short man of approximately five-feet-three inches followed this canine with steady yet quick steps.

He placed his hand on his thin lips as he exclaimed with wide eyes that were large and set deeper into his skull, creating the illusion of a more prominent brow bone.

"My! What do we have here?" he proclaimed, squinting his eyes, putting wrinkles on his bronzed-color skin as he saw Jay lying unconscious in the boat and walked quickly to rescue him.

He pushed the hair off the human's face and noticed it was stiff and rough. Jay's skin was pale and had lacerations on his forehead and cheeks that were visible in spite of the stubble. His lips were chapped. His orange life jacket was faded, and the rims along the shoulder of his jacket were uneven and disjointed.

He picked up his one hand and noticed it had blemishes. Having never realized the fury of the ocean until now, he felt sorry for this human. He picked him up from his waist while placing his one arm over him and dragged him under the trees in the shade holding the arm that was on his shoulder. He noticed his pants were ripped too while his shoes were wet and soggy.

The action of walking made Jay open his eyes partially. He looked around, and then gave a side glance to his aid. The helper paused for a bit wanting to make a conversation, "Hi, can you walk?"

"No! No, I can't walk on water," Jay said in a fearful tone shaking his head from left to right while trying to open his eyes to get a sense of his surroundings.

"No worries," said the helper lifting him up from the waist and walking briskly toward the shade of the tree. At that moment, Jay grabbed the helper's shoulder tightly, feeling bumps there making him realize the helper is burly and muscular.

As he gently placed him under the tree, Jay held onto his helper with fear thinking he is being placed on another boat, gently letting go of his grip from his shoulder that actually was creating friction on the helper's skin. But the helper was patient as he waited for him to let go completely while he was eyeing him with compassion.

Once Jay's buttocks touched something, he let go. Jay quickly started looking for support to hold onto something. He was still in a daze, so with eyes partially shut, he moved his hands rapidly. "Wait... wait, please don't row the boat yet. I want to hold onto something."

The helper could not resist knowing he had to bring him out of this trance. He held his hands gently and placed them on the ground in the sand. Jay's fingers were feeling that texture as he frowned. He blinked rapidly to remove whatever was in his eyes and opened them wide and stared down. "Am I..." he looked up, "... am I on land?" he asked in an emotional tone, then without waiting for his answer, he looked around and saw Yogi sitting next to him. Going on his fours, he played with the sand on the ground with his fingers before crawling around as if to get that assurance, and then with both his hands, he hugged Yogi and cried hard. Yogi would woof occasionally, but it was mostly Jay whose voice was heard loud and intense.

That noise drew many of people toward him, but Jay continued to cry. His cry was to celebrate his second chance at life. His howling was to protest against what happened. His sobbing was to jeer at destiny for making him see such a day!

While bawling, he kept playing with the sand in his fingers and did not care whether it got into his clothes, shoes, and hair. He was just happy to be surrounded by nature that was immovable, green, and alluring and not suffocating him to death. He glanced at the ocean, and at first was petrified, then twitched his nose giving a dirty look at it and the boat that brought them here. The humans who were standing at a distance were curious and inquired from the man who helped Jay get out of the collapsible boat.

Once those inquisitive eyes, twitching eyebrows, and fingers pointing to him became plenty, Jay got a hold of himself. He wiped his tears and tried listening but did not understand a word. The folks were speaking in a language that was foreign to him. He checked out their attire. They were bare-chested with just a skirt made either of husks of a tree while some had leaves sewn together and were wearing a necklace that had oysters as a pendant which was held with the string of a coconut.

The men were well-built with toned muscles and had tanned bronze skin just like the person who helped him off the boat. He glanced at that helper who was actually dressed differently from the others. He was wearing a pair of blue shorts made of cotton fibers unlike the others, however, he was shirtless and wearing a necklace with a unique pendant that he could not figure out even after squinting hard at it. Jay was in for another shock of his life.

The last thing he wanted was to be surrounded by people who would not understand him. Again, he feared for his life. He looked around and saw that the boat which he cursed and the ocean he damned were his only options to get out of here in one piece. He eyed his pet that was surprisingly at ease while he continued to dig around with his paws and play with small vegetation, sniffing it and jumping around.

*Yogi is so happy. He cannot sense the danger we are in,* Jay thought to himself as small trickles of sweat were forming on his forehead.

Just then, the man in blue shorts approached him with a coconut. Jay became defensive, hiding his face with his hands, thinking he is going to hurt him. But instead, "Here, drink this," he said in a sympathetic tone that showed the earnestness in his almond eyes and olive skin.

"Huh," Jay's eyes were wide as he froze.

"Aren't you thirsty? Drink this while my family is making food, and then we can all eat together," he said with a gentle smile that showed off his thick lips which, when extended, showed off his pearly whites. His words were clear. His language was comprehensible and coherent.

That made him frown. *Am I hallucinating?* he wondered. Then he nodded his head to shake off the idea that these people are strangers and quickly took the coconut from him.

Yogi was also drinking water from a dried-up coconut shell that one of the men gave him. Jay was quick to gulp it down by placing it over his mouth and drinking from it. A straw to drink through was the last thing on his mind.

He placed it next to him and asked, "How much?"

This was the time for the man in blue shorts to show confusion. "Huh?" he questioned with a frown. Jay did not have the bandwidth to repeat, so he took out a few notes from his jacket pocket. They were moist, but currency never loses value.

He stretched it toward him. "I don't have much money. But, I promise that when I reach home, I will mail you a check. So, until then, please accept this."

"This is of no use here," the man in blue shorts said, shaking his hands and head at the same time.

"No use?" Jay was shocked, then after a pause, he said, "Okay... okay. I get you. This currency is not accepted here.

Which country am I in? Is that the Pacific Ocean?" he asked, pointing at the water, not sure himself since he was in a semi-conscious state.

"Yes, Pacific Ocean," he confirmed.

"Then, I am curious which country this is that does not take U.S. dollars?" he asked with a confused look, arching his head. "But don't worry, U.S. dollars have lots of value. You can get it exchanged from your local bank," he said, extending two five-dollar notes.

"No, you don't understand," the man said in an amusing tone. "We don't use money on this island."

Jay's eyes were wide as he got another shock. "What?" he exclaimed. "You guys don't use money?" he repeated. "How do you survive?" he inquired in a sarcastic tone that was followed by a smirk.

"Survive? We live very comfortably," he said with a wide smile. "By the way, my name is McKinley. You can call me Mack." He extended his hand, and the two men shook hands in a delicate manner given the bruises on Jay's hand.

"Come, let's go. We have medicinal herbs that can help treat your bruises."

"Are you sure?" Jay hesitated. "I mean now that you don't take money, how can I pay you back for all the hospitality that I will receive until I leave?" Jay sounded confused.

"We work together. Whatever we earn, we eat and enjoy. You, too, can be a part of this... that is, as long as you want to stay here." Mack was frank and sounded optimistic.

The sun had set. There was a slight chill in the air, but it was a pleasant evening given the month of November in the Pacific Ocean. The coconut trees were swaying along giving music to the quiet and peaceful evening. Jay and Yogi walked with ginger steps toward the huts made of thatch and bundles of grass that were lined side by side. There were fire torches everywhere. He saw the same men who were inquiring about his welfare to Mack when he had an outburst of emotion upon discovering land. They were sitting around the fire sharing food from various plates. There were a handful of women too who were sitting along the side eating and chuckling. All were talking to each other, and it sounded alien to him. He blinked a couple of times followed by deep breaths to get a hold of himself, hoping that it's just a delusion. Only the vibration of laughter made him comfortable since it had the sound of authenticity and trustworthiness.

Amidst the struggle within, he was not paying attention to his pet. All he was aware of was that Yogi seemed to be comfortable in the setting, making him even more pressured to understand the new ambiance. They reached a spot where one elderly man was sitting in a seiza position, kneeling on the floor folding his legs underneath his thighs while resting his buttocks on his heels. His head was adorning a hat which resembled that of a chef's hat. He had a shawl around his bare chest and a skirt made of husk from a tree. He was eating in silence. As soon as he saw Jay, he signaled him. Jay was hesitant, but Mack touched his arm and whispered, "He is my dad. Go on."

That made him step with confident strides toward him. He bowed at him with respect, to which the chief nodded his head while raising his hand to bless him and offered him a plate. There was a pause where everyone bowed to their plate in gratitude while the tribal people spoke a few words that sounded like acknowledgment for the food they were about to consume. Jay chose to fold his hands and thank the Lord with moist eyes for being able to actually sit and eat a meal that he had always taken for granted. Soon, they opened their eyes.

"Eat," he commanded with a smile that showed off his uneven but bright white teeth. Seeing food, Jay was quick to sit down and was pleased to see food of various colors on the plate that was rough yet tough. He analyzed it to find it was made of husk. He was curious to try the food since the aroma was unique and palatable, and it made his stomach churn. The bile juices had already started to secrete getting ready to digest the soon-to-be chewed-upon food.

The chief motioned his son to join them. They both exchanged a few words, which made Jay raise his eyebrows as he eyed them. Just then, he looked out for Yogi. With no sign of him, he got up with an inquiry.

Mack was quick to fill him in. "All animals eat food at the shed. One of the members took him there."

"Can I just go and take a peek at him? I want to make sure he is in good hands." He realized what he said then quickly corrected, "I mean I just want to see him."

Mack conveyed to his dad about the change in plans, and the duo went toward the animal shed. "What language do you and your dad speak?" asked a curious Jay while walking along the unpaved path with a fire torch.

"This is a native language all my people here speak," Mack said casually, hitting a few pebbles that came under his footwear made of hemp.

"How come you speak my language?"

"When I was a teen, I went to live on an island on the west side of this place. I lived with my uncle for ten years and went to school, but I finally found my peace on this island with my parents and a few people who still love to live this lifestyle."

"Who are these people besides your parents?" asked Jay with curiosity.

"Just some people who love to live this life. There are about thirty of us in all." Then he paused. "Actually, we are thirty point five." In an excited tone, he continued, "We are a big family. Now that you are here. We are thirty-one point five."

"Huh?"

"Welcome to our island!"

They reached the shed where there were geese, hens, sheep, goats, cows, and dogs.

Yogi and Jay had their own language of communication, but that language could be easily interpreted since it was the language of love and compassion.

Once satisfied, the duo started walking back. Just then, Mack paused and bent over. He removed a leaf from a plant and oozed off something gooey and white and placed it in his palm. "Here, apply this on your face and lips. It will help you heal."

"What is this?" Jay asked with a scrunched nose looking at the texture.

"Aloe vera. We have lots of plants growing here, which are medicinal herbs besides the crops for our food and clothing. I will take you on a tour tomorrow morning."

After its application, Jay felt coolness setting in versus the sting that was at first making him very uneasy. Dinner was a treat for Jay, who had experienced a lot in the last seventy-two hours after boarding a holiday cruise, then getting off it due to an accident, and finally being stranded in the ocean that was cold and raw. All this had stripped off his aspirations for the future while he was in a collapsible boat fighting for his life.

He relished the food, and even though it was different from what he usually would nibble on, he enjoyed every bit of it. The spices were fresh, the vegetables were crisp, and their freshness actually made him feel energetic and invigorated after ingesting them. They all pitched in to clean up, and then they all sat in a big circle around the fire. There was some discussion amongst the tribal people in serious and somber tones. That was followed by singing and dancing while a couple played the drums. Jay's senses were captivated as he clapped along but was a little shy to show his dance moves, *yet!*

Gradually, the tribal people started dispersing for bedtime. Mack took charge of Jay and walked him to a small one-room shelter. He made sure Jay was comfortable on the bed that was cemented and then layered with goose feathers and dried grass. He gave him a sheet that was of goose feathers stitched together along with a pillow comprised of rolled jute to support his neck.

He was quick to remove his ripped jacket. He placed his hand over its pocket to make sure the wallet is in place, and then carefully folded it and put it aside. He was still having a hard time understanding the concept of no money on this island and had many questions for Mack but chose to keep them for the next day. The bed looked rigid and bare, but when Jay lay on it, he forgot all about comfort since the fact that destiny managed to find him land amidst the wide stretch of water. It made his eyes moist, and he felt grateful that he got away from the direct fury of Mother Nature. His body was tired, making his eyes shut when all of a sudden, he pulled his jacket close to him and snuck it under him. "Can't trust them, yet," he whispered and soon was in la-la land.

# CHAPTER TWENTY-TWO

*"You never lose by loving. You always lose by holding back." —*
*__Barbara De Angelis__*

Morning came early for Jay once the rooster cock-a-doodle-doo chimed out. The cows mooed, and the lambs bleated while the dogs and cats gave out their own sounds. He woke up with a start since he was used to a particular chime each morning. The jacket was crumpled as he lay over it. He was quick to first assess the jacket's pocket prior to wearing it, then quickly put on his shoes. Holding his bladder, he walked out with the hope to relieve it. He met some tribal people walking by his simple-roofed shelter. Seeing his body language, one of them waved him to follow them, and they walked toward a section where they had single-unit rooms built of dried grass and a jute door. While walking, he could not help but admire the beauty surrounding him.

The sun had not only painted the sky orange, but even the landscape was wearing different colors. Amongst the many trees that he did not know the names of, he was able to identify banyan trees, mango trees, and palms swaying gently to the breeze as if giving music to the surroundings. The paths were man-made, uneven but clean. There were similar huts along the way with some clay pots, dresses, and shirts made of hemp drying on a string. When they reached their destination, the tribal person picked up a tumbler of water, handed it over to Jay, and using sign language, showed him the way. Jay scrunched his nose at first, then tightened the belt of his pants to stop that urge and was walking away when Mack came by.

"Hey, this is our toilet system here. We don't have flush toilets, and the dump that we all excrete goes into making manure for our plantations. So, go ahead." He ushered him toward a single unit that had a raised seating courtesy of wooden blocks placed in four corners. It had a big, wide hole on top.

At first, Jay could not stand the thought of no-flush toilets, so he walked away. While strolling toward his hut, he experienced the cramps in his stomach and intestines which made him falter a bit, and he tried to reason within.

*The space is clean. No mosquitoes. It's the concept that is difficult to digest. Well, Jay, you have no choice, so just go for it.* His mind talked to his heart, and then with raised eyebrows and a twitched nose, he turned toward the toilets.

Mack had just finished his job and was washing his hands. Seeing him come back, he smiled and could not resist, "When you have to go, you have to go."

Jay blushed and walked to that chamber, shut the door that was made of sheer jute, and soon he was out wearing a relieved look. Mack introduced him to soap and a bucket of water instead of running water that he was used to in his urban living. And then there was coconut oil for brushing his teeth.

"Welcome to the medieval age, my friend," Mack humored, twitching his nose. "After breakfast, I will give you a tour of this island which should take a few hours."

"I'm famished. But first, I have to go visit Yogi."

Yogi was busy with the farm animals. He was frolicking around with them, but when he saw his master, he rushed to him like a child goes to his dad after daycare. They shared some fond moments. Jay asked him questions, and he responded with licks and tail wagging that was at the speed of twenty miles per hour. Soon the caretaker called out to him and placed a plate on the ground. Yogi gave a final woof to his master and rushed at it. Jay was very happy seeing Yogi and his contentment.

He looked around to see hemp plants growing in abundance to which Mack was quick to respond, almost reading his mind, "We use hemp products so we make sure we plant plenty of them."

"Yes, I have been observing," Jay said with appreciation. As they walked back toward the huts, he could smell various odors of medicaments and saw the various plants of herbs around. "Would you like to take a shower and then apply aloe vera for your cuts?" the tribal inquired.

"Oh, please, I don't want to go near water for some time. I don't mind the application of gel, though, since I see promising results from last night."

When he approached the huts, his stomach started rumbling thanks to the aroma. He entered the paved area that led to a chamber. It consisted of many stoves and a shed where grains and food were stored. There was porridge made of wheat husk and milk along with fresh fruits and wheat bread baked in the clay oven with dollops of home-made butter on it. Jay first bowed to all and then sat on the floor while rubbing his hands with apprehension.

The porridge was served in a palm bowl and the other food on a palm plate. Some would eat with their hands or just slurp it, making an unusual noise, which was disturbing to Jay, having had a life with forks and spoons. Again, the vibes were cordial. He felt it beyond a family since there was no competition of any sort. The tribal people's body language was very docile, and they were amicable with each other's habits. He took a deep breath and continued to satisfy his hunger. After washing and cleaning their hands, Mack started the tour of the island for Jay.

At first, they passed by the lodging huts, and then the arcade of herbs and fruit trees and various other trees whose names sounded foreign to him as Mack was describing them to him. The trees stretched for over a mile, and then came the single units of toilets followed by the barn where animals were resting. Thereafter, they reached the stretch of fields where they were growing crops. He could recognize the wheat and rice crops thanks to his granddad's fields in India while he just nodded when his guide pointed to them. They were also growing vegetables on the far end, and stretches of banyan trees were dividing these two fields.

The island seemed small since he could see the mountains at the other end. "Thanks to those volcanic mountains, our soil is fertile while we have our own ways to make manure for our plants and crops."

"Volcano!" Jay's eyes widened. "Is it active?"

"The last time it erupted was about a hundred or so years ago according to the geologists who visited when this land was discovered. The soil is still rich with its minerals."

"So, how can I help?" Jay sounded enthusiastic, rubbing his hands. "Be my helper?"

"Sounds exciting."

"For the past few days, I have been tending to the crops since it's harvest time." He walked toward the fields and got to work. At first, Jay was a little hesitant of the dirt, but then realized how effortlessly Mack was doing his chores. He got down on his knees, but still he had many questions.

"So, how is it your uncle lives on a commercial island while your parents chose to live here?"

"It is just a matter of choice, my friend. My dad and some of his male friends had gone fishing years back and discovered this desolate island. The black soil attracted them to spend the night here. He and his friends discovered the potential of this island, went back home, and announced to the folks there of their intentions to move to the island. Many agreed, and they rowed their boats here. Gradually, life here grew. This land has been in dispute over the U.S. and Japanese territory, so no government wanted to invest in it. These folks brought seeds and started life on this island. However, life without electricity and many comforts including the flushed toilets cannot be lived without, so a handful of them left. By that time, I was born. I lived here until age ten. I had a lot of questions and was also curious about life on other islands since I would sometimes visit with my dad to get the essential commodities such as lye for the soap, sharp tools for cutting and chopping. I then became curious about life on those islands."

He pointed yonder. "My dad insisted I go see that part of the world since he wanted me to make a choice when I was old enough. I went and lived with my uncle for a few years, studied in a school there, learned this language, and saw that part of life, including money. I have also done transactions with money, but there was something within that made me come back. So, here I am," he said with a wide smile. His eyes were twinkling as if the constellation was right there in him. He had a special warmth in his aura that made Jay want to know more, but a tribal woman who asked Mack to do a chore interrupted them.

At first, he was very excited and jumped in joy, then responded to her in their tribal language and rushed in a different direction, leaving Jay clueless. This California guy just stood there baffled as to which direction to go. At that moment, he felt homesick since he had no clue what they said and why the sudden reaction.

He initially thought he would just sit there and sulk over it, then looked at the crops that Mack was working on, so he continued to cut down the harvested wheat crop.

Soon, he got busy, and little did he realize Mack was standing next to him. "Hi, we are having a little baby on this island," he said with joy.

"Okay!" Jay was not amused but smiled.

"Remember, I told you we are thirty point five in total population. This point five is now going to be a single individual. I was told to get the father from the fields while my mom and other ladies help with the delivery."

That made Jay jump up. "What do you mean delivery? Aren't they going to take her to the hospital?"

Mack looked around. "Which hospital? Where? It is just us. And these women are well trained in birthing. We have all the medicinal herbs, and they know the procedure. Let's just wait for the good news," he said, wiping his hands off his sleeveless shirt that showed off his toned muscles.

Jay eyed them secretly, especially since he was a tall, lanky guy. Mack was quick to catch the glimpse and could not resist in commenting, "If you do all this labor work as I do, you, too, will be toned in no time!" His blunt flat nose literally spread all over his face when he smiled. Jay blushed at first then raised his eyebrows, confused over the earlier discussion. He continued, "How do you get general commodities from other islands? You don't have money, so how do you do transactions?"

"Barter system, my friend. We take our produce from here. Sell it or trade it on that island. And come back with our necessities."

"I can imagine your dad must be making all these decisions?" an impressed Jay inquired.

"All the tribal people have a say, actually. No doubt my dad is the chief, but he has an ear open for all," Mack said, continuing to chop down the crops.

"Lucky you," Jay whispered while performing the same actions as Mack upon the crop of wheat.

There was a pause, and then Mack inquired, "So tell me about yourself?"

Jay was reluctant to disclose his past yet, so he mentioned, his decision to go on a holiday and then the shipwreck followed by how he and his pet got away from the rest of the passengers.

"Aha! Glad you made it safe, huh?" Mack blinked, trying to bring humor to his grim mood to which Jay did not show much amusement. He chose to keep quiet. Mack was persistent to bring that smile, so he inquired about his past.

"Your parents or loved ones would be curious to know about your welfare. When we go to the island in a few days, you could call them from there or even board a flight back home."

"Nah! I don't think anyone would be keen to know about it."

"What do you mean?" The above comment concerned Mack as he asked in a serious tone.

Jay took a deep breath and sat down cross-legged. "My dad left his duties of being a father, a husband, and a son many years ago when he chose to walk away from us all. After many years, my fiancée broke off with me, and here I am!"

"Okay, so?" Mack asked in a very matter-of-fact tone, shocking Jay, who was expecting empathy from him.

He turned toward him with a frown, but Mack was relentless. "Don't you have any friends whom you would want to inform or maybe your mom?"

# CHAPTER TWENTY-THREE

*"Be smart, be strong, be proud, live honorably and with dignity, and just hold on."*
— *James Frey*

Jay got another opportunity to go into his shell. "My mom is busy managing the empire built by my granddad and dad."

"Oh, good for her," Mack said in a genuine tone while continuing to chop down the crops and bundling them in groups. "But she is your mom first, then a businesswoman. She must be worried, huh?"

"With the way I have treated her, I think she is better off without me around her." Jay chose not to answer the question directly.

Mack raised his eyebrow, curious to know more, so he continued, "I have a cousin whom we adopted when she lost her parents in an accident. Her mother was my dad's sister." He paused to see his reaction.

Mack was nodding with a gentle smile. "Wow, you got to grow up with a sibling in spite of your dad walking out on you all."

Jay was dazzled at how he could connect the dots. That made him smile and also encouraged him to go on. "Yes! She was a blessing since she was not only my confidante in all my problems as a teen, but she is also my best friend. In fact, I have left my café in her hands while I was supposed to be on my holiday." These words made Jay's tone somber, but Mack was quick to pick it up from there. "See, so you ought to tell her that you and Yogi are safe, right?"

Jay nodded in agreement. After being shipwrecked and seeing death so close, he had become needy for love and destitute for closure since he did not trust time. Time was never his friend since it always made him bump into a dead end. He was worried it would throw him again in turmoil, and he feared he might not be able to come out of it. So, he was curious to know Mack's take about his dad leaving, so he went back to that topic.

"You know I was very close to my dad. We were like best buddies until he decided to go to the mountains. Something changed within him when Gina's parents passed away. He was a recluse for a month or two, then he came out of it a totally changed person. He coaxed my mom to join him at work and trained her for a couple of months while I was busy basking in my newfound sibling, Gina. Then after a month or two, he went off on a pilgrimage with my grandparents, followed by a family holiday with just Mom, Gina, and me with him. I never noticed the changes since I was busy quarreling with Gina, or sharing, smiling, and playing while my parents spent quality time together. But I vividly remember now and then that my dad would talk to me about responsibility and maturity, but honestly, I did not understand a bit. Maybe because of my teen years." He shrugged his shoulders and rumpled his lips. Mack was sitting and listening attentively.

"Then he made the announcement. Everything came to a standstill. My grandparents were shocked. My mom could not stop crying while Gina and I thought it to be a joke." He chuckled with moist eyes.

"Why would you take that as a joke? "Mack asked.

"A joke because who can give up everything, go to the mountains, and live in solitude?" Then Jay paused. "I mean not exactly live in solitude since I have heard there are many such people out there living a meditative life," he said while rubbing his hands against each other trying to assure himself of his thoughts.

"That's understandable for your dad to do," Mack said in a concerned tone.

"Understandable? What my dad did? What are you saying?" Jay said in a disrespectful tone.

Mack went on to justify himself. "No doubt what your dad did was not right. He ought to take care of his duties first as a dad and husband. But from what I understand after listening to all that you said earlier, he didn't just go off. He trained your mom to keep the household running while you were enjoying Gina's company." Then after a pause, he said, "Well, each soul is different and has a right to do what he or she desires. Your dad realized the deeper meaning of life after he lost his sister and her husband. He wanted to live a more meaningful one. Peeling off the layers of his personal life one at a time, he finally then went for nirvana!"

"You are talking as we were just the mere onion in his life that made him cry." Jay moved his head from left to right in disgust.

"Talking about peels, I believe they make fries out of potatoes by peeling it into thin slices, too. And they are yum!" There was a twinkle in his eyes as he continued, "So, now we can't just compare ourselves to onions, huh?"

Jay sneered at the above comment before taking a breath and started tying the bundles together with a jute rope.

"So, you seriously think what my dad did was correct?" Jay could not help but ask him directly.

"Who am I to judge? It's where his soul found happiness. Moreover, he did not leave you guys on the road. Did he? You are talking about business and empire, so I guess you had all the comforts that money could find."

"But what about growing up with a father? I lost one as a teen, dammit," Jay said as he got up on his feet and threw a twig in the air with the hopes it would swing far, but it landed near his feet. He felt his temper fizzle out instantaneously looking at the darn branch.

"I can understand where you're going with it, Jay..." Mack spoke with tenderness, "... but it was his idea of leaving, and nothing can be done about it. So why try to peel the past and dissect it further? Let the past be the past. You move on, especially after life has given you a second chance to live." There was silence.

"Now seriously, Jay, you should inform your cousin about your survival when we go to the island. I will keep you informed."

That was followed by a long silence since Jay was contemplating Mack's opinions while the latter was just busy. Soon an announcement was made. Mack sprung up and translated it for his friend, "It's a boy," he exclaimed, looking at Jay while he sprung around restlessly trying to clean up before dashing toward the little baby just to hold him.

There was a pail of water that everyone used to clean their hands before holding the baby, and everyone took turns to coo him. Jay just stood at a distance while keeping a steady smile. Mack was observing from a distance. Then he made an announcement to his tribal family to which they all agreed, and then Mack shouted out to Jay, "Jay, propose a name for the baby."

"What?" He was surprised and confused.

"Yes, you heard it right. My tribal family would like you to name this baby. The parents want a name, Jay." He looked at the father of the baby and then shifted his glance at the newcomer.

Jay was still baffled as he opened his eyes and mouth wide to show his perplexity, but Mack was persistent along with the tribal people who were looking at him with curious eyes.

That's when he realized they were serious, "Umm... Mack, can you give me some time to think?"

"Sure."

Jay wandered away while deep in thought. He was reminiscing the time when he and his dad spent moments together, thanks to the pictures clicked and saved by his mom. The black and white photographs consisted of the horseback riding on his dad's back, the camel ride on his dad's shoulders, the laying on his dad's chest and sleeping for hours, and the weird faces he and his father used to make. He remembered vividly those long lectures he gave him about responsibilities and looking after his mom while he snoozed off from boredom. He even remembered the day when his dad announced he was leaving his family for the mountains, the goodbyes, and the promise he and Gina made that he will come running to his comfortable mattress, and the warm down comforter. He giggled, remembering them while tears were trickling down his eyes. He went toward his hut and sat on his bed, deep in thought, allowing the tears to roll down freely. He did not notice Mack at his doorstep until he made a noise of clearing his throat.

"Hey!"

"I have thought of the name for the baby," Jay said with excitement wiping his tears.

"It's the God of Wind. I name him Anil."

"Wow!"

"Let's go and inform the rest," Mack said with joy while Jay followed him with quick steps. Jay washed his hands. Held the one-hour old baby in his arms and said it out loud, "Anil." Mack interpreted the meaning of the name in the tribal language, and that was followed by a loud cheer!

********

Evening came early and so did the celebrations. Food was a gala affair after they had taken some time to show their gratitude to the Lord. Sweets and music and lots of dancing followed food. Jay was amazed that even though they lived an uncluttered lifestyle, they could fit sweets in their lives. Jay felt one amongst them and did not hesitate to show his moves this time. He felt somewhat lighter and liberated but could not figure out the reason behind it. It just made him want to laugh, be amongst company, and eat his heart out. He even slept well that night despite talking at length about his past. He woke up next morning courtesy of the music chimed by the farm animals with his jacket close to him as he still wanted to guard the money in it. He was in awe of what happened last night. No chills or nightmares! Then he tried to reason it out. *Maybe it's the work in the sun and then the dance and music, thanks to his only English-speaking buddy.*

He continued to be Mack's helper, and today's itinerary involved laying out the bundles of wheat to dry, and then picking the ripe vegetables which meant hopping from one aisle of the field to another to scan and pick.

"So, don't you get bored of this farm life?" Jay inquired as he plucked the cabbage and placed it in a container.

"Why should I? This is my livelihood." Mack smiled, then after a pause inquired about his vocation back home to which Jay responded with fervor describing his unique café which serves tea and snacks, and went on to explain how he remembers all his customers' orders while trying to show that he is a people person.

"Don't you get bored of serving tea to the same faces?" Mack asked curiously to which Jay was taken aback at first, but he loved Mack's honesty and chuckled over it, nodding from left to right appreciating his sense of humor.

"You are witty, my friend!" he remarked. Mack took it as a compliment.

"So, are you in touch with your mom?" a curious Mack inquired while busy with the produce.

Jay froze over that question and fell quiet. Mack was in no rush. He waited patiently for him to answer, not speaking anything further while Jay was dreading to answer, especially with the kind of treatment he had given his mom ever since his dad had left. Guilt was building up within, pushing him to take forever to respond. Mack would look up now and then just to indicate that he was waiting for a response while Jay was trying to choose words just to get the right ones out. "I have been busy," he said in a hushed tone.

Mack was appreciative of what he heard, nodding with raised eyebrows, "Sure. Running a café is not easy. I get that."

That made Jay frown. *Who is this person? Sometimes he is taking my side, and sometimes he is just the opposite,* he mulled over.

Soon, they were carrying the vegetables to the main hut where dining and cooking occurred. The labor made him sweat, but he refused to take off his jacket.

"You have transacted money and now no transaction at all. How do you feel about it?" a curious Jay asked, wiping his sweat off his forehead.

"Money for me is paper. Money for me is the produce I carry to the other island to obtain what my family or I need here on the island." Mack was very clear about it.

"But what if you have to go to civilization? Won't you need this paper to survive? So, why not save up and stack them under your bed or something?"

"I have the knowledge that will get me that paper, my friend. This expertise on how to farm and harvest will get me a job, and eventually, that paper to buy me food. So, why waste time to keep stacking it under my pillow?"

"That's a valid point," Jay said in an impressive tone with a smile that was so wide that it felt like the crescent shape of the moon.

Life on the island was going smoothly for Jay, even though he would at times scratch his skin or have bruises while doing the farm work. What made it heal so fast was the affection and consideration of the tribal people. The ritual of serving him a concoction of turmeric as an antiseptic and reminding him to bandage it regularly would give him goosebumps.

He would wake up after a sound sleep of eight hours and be as fresh as a daisy. His mind and body were in tune with the surroundings as he would notice how civil and cordial the tribal people would be to each other and to him. He was already a part of their family as he would see Anil each day getting stronger by the hour with the love and caring hands of thirty-one people around him. He is the first baby of this island, and they all love him as if he is theirs.

Jay felt that love rise within as he remembered how his grandparents and mom would pamper him and Gina when his dad opted for the hills. He never really understood it since he was still mourning the loss of his dad's presence, although he and Gina would bet on his arrival secretly each month. Each would take turns to bet. *'He is coming back by the end of this month,'* but there was no winner since he never came back. Life went on until Jay left for college for his master's in business management in the US, and Gina for her Masters in the West Indies, Jamaica.

Today Jay was seeing that same kind of unadulterated love, and it made him relive those moments of his life that he had developed a shield against. Blame it on anger and frustration to answer those taunts when nasty teens would inquire about his dad in a hostile way.

His heart had shattered from the plethora of hostile incidents by teens his age, but the love and care of the people on this island gave that heart an opportunity to heal as his heart absorbed their affection and tenderness. He could feel the thump of the blood-pumping organ getting stronger, and that also gave a boost to his confidence. He, along with the others, would take turns to play with the baby whom he had grown fond of. It could be due to the name or the mere mischief of the infant, but unknowingly the name was giving him closure.

*******

"Hey, wake up, sleepyhead." An early knock on his door forced Jay to open his eyes rather unwillingly.

These days his jacket would be lying in one corner of that room with the wallet still zipped into it. The fondness to the people on the island and the trust toward them made him take the jacket off his body since he was assured that the stack of paper that has US presidents' pictures are of no use to them.

"We have enough produce to go to the island for a trade-off. Why don't you join us so that you can inform your family? Before that, we have an early breakfast meeting

174

today. Please join us."

"An early breakfast meeting? What's up?" Jay was inquisitive.

"You will know soon."

Jay freshened up his usual way since the clothing he was wearing was all he had. So, after the usual use of the toilet, he would wash his private parts and scrub his face using tumblers of water and then style his hair with his stubby fingers while massaging the stubbles along his cheek and upper lip. *How I wish I could shave and wear fresh, clean clothes,* sniffing his underarms to make sure he is devoid of any odor.

*Oh, I know they are going to the island. My stack of paper will come in handy to buy me what I need.* He grinned at his idea and was quick to wear his jacket.

When he met everyone at the breakfast hut, Mack wore a frown when he saw him in the jacket. Along with a frown, he was also wearing a sling bag that was made of leather courtesy of one of his purchases from the island. He used it to carry all his essentials prior to starting his trip off the island. Today was the day. Jay was confused seeing his reaction as his eyebrows twitched but chose to ignore it and did not inquire. Before breakfast came the announcement where all tribal people were supposed to give their list of needs for after the trade-off with the produce, the men will shop before coming back home.

Jay was excited and the first to raise his hand to give his list that Mack made a note of. It included clothes and a razor. Satisfied, Jay sat with a perfect smile as he waited to hear the others' needs and was shocked that all of them thought of the baby and his needs rather than their personal urgencies. He was embarrassed and felt guilty.

After giving their thanks, they all had breakfast, and then all the adults pitched in to load their two boats with the immense amount of produce they had harvested. Two boats were a big deal for this tribe. All were happy with the fact that they could double their production within six months of their last visit to the nearby island. Singing and laughing were in accompaniment as all helped load the boats while Mack and two other tribal men were getting last-minute orders from their tribal head *a.k.a.* Mack's dad. Jay had gone to say hello and goodbye to his Yogi who seemed to have bonded well with the farm animals.

While the activity of loading was going on, Mack went toward the shore with a bundle of rope when he noticed a certain reflection on the waters. Confused, he looked around and saw nobody in sight. Then some urgency caught him within. He gasped for breath as if someone was choking him. He was walking helter-skelter at first, then was quick to get behind a palm tree and rest while taking heavy and deep breaths, and pulled out his spyglass from his sling bag and looked in the direction of the reflection. All he could see was a glare courtesy of the sun's rays.

He panicked again and called out to his tribal folk to which they were quick to take cover. The boats were standing alone on the shore while all the men and women were talking in hushed tones. Jay came back to see the boats alone and was surprised. He looked around to see them all either behind the bark of the trees or just kneeling on all fours. At first, he became very confused, then thought it must be some ritual before their departure, so he just went and sat on a rock while noticing they were talking with a frown on their foreheads. Very confused, he chose to stay out of it. Mack saw him and called out his name in an urgent tone. Jay frowned and nodded his head because he was worried he would be asked to say some words of wisdom which he had no clue, so just nodded his head from left to right refusing to come to him.

"Jay, come here now! It is urgent," Mack said in an outraged tone. Now that had him very confused and also worried. He was quick to run toward him. Mack pushed him on the sand while he was kneeling on all fours.

He was startled by the sudden moves, and before he could express it, Mack said, "Somebody is watching us. We have to be vigilant."

Then he pointed his spyglass in that direction and showed him. The sight that lay before his eyes made Jay gulp hard, really hard since that damn saliva refused to go in.

"What do we do? They could be pirates," Jay said with wide eyes and a heartbeat so loud he could not hear Mack.

"Slow down," Mack urged, placing his hand on his shoulder. "It could just be another ship looking for land. But, we ought to be cautious," he said with a pensive smile while looking at his tribal brethren who were communicating as well.

He took another glance with his hand-held telescope and could not find anything. The coast seemed clear. He took in a deep sigh of relief and announced it to his tribal folks. They cheered while getting up, and that was enough for Jay to cheer along too.

*Amazing how, when expressed, happiness and sorrow have no language barriers.*

He cheered along with them while giving out a big sigh of relief and pacing himself on the sandy beach allowing his heart to beat at a regular pace.

"See, I told you. It was just a random boat," Mack bragged. "We have had many such happenings, but we have to be sure to be on the watch out for the safety of my brethren." He grinned.

Soon all activities went back to normal. They all started loading their boats with sacks of wheat and corn. They also had baskets of assorted vegetables and fruits and different herbs that were crushed and finely packaged in small jute bags. Mack was expecting a lot of goods via the barter system, however, they had to load two boats because four people were going to the island, and they had plans of staying two nights to make sure they sell everything on the boats.

Jay was looking forward to this trip with the hopes he could connect with his cousin and also get some new clothing for himself. He proudly patted his pocket. *Jeez, living here will help me lose my love for money. The zeal to make money is what has kept me busy.* He grinned.

# CHAPTER TWENTY-FOUR

*"You might not want to burn your bridges when you're standing on an island."*
— *Jennifer Niven*

Back home, Gina was getting restless, fidgety, and irritated over every minuscule thing as she was losing hope over Jay's homecoming, especially since his car was towed back to his address. It broke her heart, but she kept assuring herself that it's just a car. She had not texted or been in touch with her grandparents and Jay's mom with the pretext that she was extremely busy. She would snap at her customers if they would take too long to decide on their order or even taunt the instructors if they would be late or not help with the cleaning.

Sam was observing all this from a distance and would now and then bring in his extinguisher to calm the fires that she had started via her anger and agitation over time ticking away and no respite in the air. She would often curse fate and would mock at herself with moist eyes over the words of wisdom she used to pour out to her cousin. Today, she mocked all that gibberish as she was convinced that life does not offer a second chance. She did not care who the audience would be. At times, she broke down in the middle of a ceramic class halting everything since there were no words to console her. Word was spreading like fire about

Jay missing in action.

Old customers would swing by to either console her or inquire further. Gina's mood swings would keep everyone at a distance since no words were the 'right words' of consolation that she would bow thee with thanks. She was getting either agitated over it or just bawled over it like a child whose toys have been forcefully taken away.

One evening, Sam held her back over some accounting issues she used to take pride upon, embarrassing her, when he pointed out the calculation error. Hassled and confused, she sat with the books in the kitchen while he secretly had food delivered from her favorite restaurant, Lorenzo's Italian Diner, and set up the table with candles. He locked the café from inside with a closed sign and turned up the volume of Adele, her favorite artist, *Hello.*

Her velvety voice made Gina jump off her seat as she was prompt to walk out the kitchen into the café. Seeing the surroundings made her heart flutter, and she couldn't help but giggle like a teen. She felt special. She felt wanted, and after what she was going through emotionally, she just walked into the café and sang the lyrics while holding Sam's hand, beckoning him to dance with her. Sam was delighted to see her reaction and went along. They danced to *One and Only* and *Set Fire to the Rain,* and then Sam took her to the table where the house salad, Alfredo chicken pasta, fried calamari, and lasagna along with crescents and red wine were waiting to be consumed. She was bewildered at his planning and did not hesitate to give him a peck on his cheek while clapping her hands in delight.

Sam took this opportunity to take their relationship to the next level by giving her a French kiss. The kiss with a tongue stimulated Gina's lips, tongue, and mouth, and she was quick to participate in this slow, passionate kiss. She closed her eyes while her eyebrows twitched, and she stood on her toes given her short height, but as they continued the process of tongue touching, she seemed to relax, and there was an endorphin release within her reducing her stress level. That helped to ease her as the lines on her forehead disappeared, and she was blushing while being motionless to keep the kissing from being uninterrupted.

All the while, Sam caressed her ears, her cheeks, and neck. When Sam's lips parted, her eyes were still shut as if she were hanging on to the moment. After a few seconds, she sat on her chair while Sam served her. She had a big, wide smile on her lips, and her eyes were dreamy as she continued to sway with the background music. Sam handed her a tall glass of wine.

"*To us.*" He brought forward his glass to which she clinked and repeated, "*To us,*" in an affirmative tone. They continued to sip in silence. Sam wanted her to be in this moment, and from Gina's look, she too wanted time to halt. They ate each course very slowly. Intending to keep her stress subdued, Sam massaged her shoulders accompanied by affectionate kisses. She was needy for love and affection.

The action made their stomachs growl making them giggle at first and then continuing to be wrapped in each other's arms, they fed themselves and each other. Gina would halt now and then as if contemplating over their interaction. Sam was quick to explain, "I have always wanted to take our relationship to the next level. I'm not embarrassed, so why should you be? You know I am in for keeps regarding us."

Gina blushed while she gingerly played with her food.

Sam kept eyeing her while giving her space. Then, in an emotionally aroused tone, he said, "I love you, Gina."

She was all pink as she stopped and stared at him with her mouth open. Then, after a couple of blinks, she chuckled while Sam continued, "I had taken a liking to you when you visited Jay the first time, but you hardly paid any attention to me. This time, I was adamant to know where we stand. And I am thrilled where we are right now."

Gina was speechless and chose to peck him on his cheek with a gentle smile.

Time was a thief, and the moist eyes would blink now and then to get that salt off, but Sam and Gina's relationship went to the next level as adversity brought them closer.

*******

Dawn had set in, and Gina realized the number of chores she had to do before opening the café as the high school teens were quite prompt in buying their morning dose of caffeine before setting into a day of learning. She gently pushed Sam away with giggles and got down to business while he sulked at first but then was quick to help her clean up. He was about to leave for his day job when Gina called out, "Thanks for a wonderful evening, Sam. Just what I needed the most, and I'm also happy to have you in my life," she said while exhibiting her pearly whites and eyes that were glistening with happiness.

Alas, that state of mind was only temporary as inquiries kept pouring in concerning Jay. Guilt took over, and she was back to being the irritated and disturbed young lady in search of answers about her cousin. Sam saw her behavior in the evening and out of despair, secretly called Jay's mom.

After giving his background information, he came to the point. At the other end, the call went blank. His heart skipped a beat hoping she did not collapse, but after repeated hellos, she announced in a restrained tone, "We are coming there."

Sam gulped and hung up. Now he was nervous to tell Gina and was trying to find ways to express it to her but with no luck. The only plus to all the chaotic happenings was that Gina and Cee-Cee were bonding. When Cee-Cee would come for her regular cup and snack, she made it a point to inquire about Jay, and that's when Gina would again pour her heart out, and they would continue to talk for another ten minutes. There were days when Cee-Cee wanted consolation and hope. That's when the tables would turn, and Gina would make sure to step in after subduing her emotions. Life was going on as usual at the Got T café. With customers pouring in and the evening classes continuing just as Jay would want, the emotions were not in the right place!

# CHAPTER TWENTY-FIVE

*"Even people capable of living in the past don't really know what the future holds."*
— <u>Stephen King</u>

Prior to their departure, the shore was crowded with the inhabitants of the island. Men, women, and even the little infant, Anil, were there. Excitement and fervor were in the air. After a short speech byAhe, Mack's dad, which included folding hands and raising them now and then, he concluded he was wishing good luck to the four crew members. Followed by a loud cheer, Mack and the other tribal men pulled out the anchor and shouted, "Ahoy!"

The two boats sailed along the Pacific Ocean. The winds were in the northeast direction, and the skies were clear with not a single cloud in sight. The blueness was sparkling amidst the bright sun, making everything so clear that any man could build up enough confidence to reach his goals. This team of four had the same feelings as they waved to the cheery crowd. Soon, they were long gone, and all the tribal people on the island could see were tiny figures at a distance while the landscape of blue ocean and blue skies remained the same. Jay drew in a deep breath as he inhaled that scenario, however, he was hoping that history didn't repeat itself with him ending up searching for land while moving his hands and feet furiously in the water.

The sailing was smooth. Mack let loose the sails to speed up the boat while blowing out a trumpet indicating to his neighboring boat to follow suit. Seeing Jay's expression, he could read his mind. "Don't worry. History never dares to repeat itself, especially when I am around," he said with a wicked smile.

Jay felt assured by that attitude and could not resist commenting, "Oh, I had forgotten you are the king of the ocean."

Mack nodded with pride. "I know every wave even before it pervades the ocean."

Mack maneuvered the boat to the right longitude and latitude toward the island. Jay could see activity from a distance and was thrilled upon seeing life and land. It was early evening when they reached their destination. Jay got goosebumps and was elated at seeing civilization in proper attire and the humdrum of city life with lights brightly shining and loud music being played through a microphone. It felt like centuries since he had seen 'normal' life.

They pulled their boats to the harbor and dropped anchor. Mack picked up two jute bags of approximately ten inches by seventeen inches and walked with steady steps toward the dock. The bags gave off a distinct aroma of cinnamon and cardamom, and Jay was quick to eye Mack while he was folding the mainsail with a jute rope. He saw his mate come back with two tickets for the boats, and after showing it to his tribal brethren, he was quick to pull out a bag. "Come, let's eat. I'm famished, and then we will camp under those palm trees for tonight."

Jay could not resist. "You got cheated. For two big bags of spices that are actually worth hundreds of dollars, you traded for tickets for two nights! You should have consulted me. Let me handle your arrangements from now on," he said while eyeing that person behind the window.

Mack was at first taken aback by his accusation, then laughed. "I have to get rid of all my produce before I go back home. So, what if he took more than he deserved. In the end, I have to consider my convenience." He grinned, but Jay was not convinced.

"You could have bought so many things out of the money you would have earned selling those bags than just trading it off for two forty-dollar tickets."

Mack had a frown and with a very serious look, said, "What would I have bought? The list of my people is meager. I never take the leftover money back to the island but usually donate it here. So, what's the use of this anger, my friend?"

"Huh? Donate?" Jay's eyes were wide like a cannonball since donations had never crossed his mind.

Leaving Jay star-struck, Mack called out to his tribal brethren as he chose a place under the trees to open the big bag of goodies that the women folks had packed for them.

After a quick wash from the nearby rest area, which was a treat for Jay as toilets flushed and water was flowing via a tap as compared to his unhurried life on the island, the four sat on the grass. Jay was there physically, but mentally he was eyeing the life that was happening at a distance on this island. His taste buds craved for something oily, something spicy, and also a warm caffeine beverage. He looked yonder where a lot was happening. He could hear live music, laughter, the clinking of glasses, and a distinctive smell that reminded him of home.

"Mack, you guys start eating. I will be back in a few minutes," he said as he patted the pocket of his jacket and walked toward that place. While walking, he realized how unkempt he was. He paused for a bit scanning himself and sniffed his underarms. But the allure in the distance had gotten to him, so he continued walking. Electricity and lights were at first constricting his eyes as he narrowed them to be able to focus. Gradually, he adjusted to them and loved being back in civilization. He was wearing something naturally, and he didn't even notice it.

A smile! He wandered around like a lost puppy. There was so much to see, so many things to taste that he stopped at one vendor who had the most delectable foods on display.

"Excuse me!" he said in an excited tone.

Her back was facing him as she was mending some things. "I will be right with you," she beckoned in an American accent. It was so pleasing to his ears as compared to hearing that strange accent he had to always stop and figure out their meaning. He smiled and looked away at other displays.

"Yes, how can I help you?" a voice inquired as she collected her long black hair and tied it in a ponytail. It accentuated her wheat-colored complexion along with her stubby nose and almond-shaped eyes. He froze with wide eyes and an open mouth. She inquired again. He could not speak, although this time he had started to blink, but nothing came out of his mouth. He was rendered speechless.

"Are you okay?" this lady inquired.

He nodded and wanted to utter yes, but no sound came out.

"Take your time to order." She was polite as she started attending to other customers.

He stood aside still trying to speak but no luck. His mind was racing with memories exhausting him completely.

Finally, he sat down in a corner. *How can this be? And she doesn't even recognize me? Do I look so different now?* He touched his face and realized the facial hair.

Time was flying by, and the contents in her stall were selling out fast. This lady called out to him once more, "Have you decided what you want, sir?"

*Sir? She calls me sir. What's wrong with her? Maybe she has lost it?*

Seeing him perplexed and confused, she brought him a plate that contained taro leaves rolled up with a filling in it. "Try this! You will love it. It's my grandmother's recipe."

The smell was alluring, so he quickly took the plate. His stomach rumbled upon inhaling the aroma, and it made him pick up the rolled-up delicacy and bite into it.

"Yummy," he exclaimed with wide eyes.

"Thank heaven you can speak now," she teased him. "That will be five dollars, please."

*What? She is asking for money from me? What about the time when she left me with all that debt to take care of?* He thought for a bit, but her constant staring made him quit that thought, and he quickly dug into his pocket.

"Will U.S. dollars do?"

"Yes." She was quick to take it and went back to her business while he devoured the food and eyed her now and then.

The food was gone in a few minutes, leaving him wanting more. He scanned the items in her stall and ordered more, paying reluctantly, though. Thanks to him and many other regular customers, her containers were soon empty, and she packed up, loading her empty trays on a tricycle cart. She had a petite frame, but she worked swiftly.

"What is your name?" he was quick to inquire this time without any inhibitions.

"Maya."

*She has changed her name too! Gosh. She sure has lost her memory. Poor girl. Maybe I should remind her of who she really is,* he thought. While he was busy gathering the guts to say his thoughts, she cycled off after collecting her long skirt together and tucking it on one side.

"Hey, wait up," he shouted, running after her, but she did not stop. She kept peddling away with a tune on her lips. Her legs were maneuvering the bike swiftly, swinging it to the left and right artistically thanks to her biceps exhibited through her short-sleeve blouse.

"Sasha, wait up," he shouted with the hope she would stop, but she continued on as smoothly as the wind brushed by him.

He felt dejected and miserable. *Why does life have to be so difficult for me? Damn,* he cursed, continuing to follow her to the best of his ability. Luckily, working in the fields had given him the stamina and strength in his legs, making him very frisky and energetic. He did not realize it until now and grinned when his body kept up with her.

Maya stopped outside a cottage, and as she was emptying the platters from her cart, she called out a name several times, "Ray." He appeared shirtless, scratching his unkempt brown hair and wearing crop pants. From his appearance, it seemed he had been sleeping, and her shouting his name woke him up. He was agitated and seemed restless as he shouted at her. She kept quiet and continued to do her chores.

Jay was observing all this from a distance curious who this person would be, and soon it became clear when a toddler came running toward her, "Mummy, I'm hungry," she cried as she carried a ragged doll in her hands. The color of her hair was similar to Ray's, while her complexion and features matched Maya's whom he kept referring to as Sasha.

Jay got the shock of his life as if he were struck by lightning, again! He stood still staring at the scenario, refusing to gulp or blink. *Is fate playing games with me or am I hallucinating?* he thought as he forced himself to sit on the footpath while trying to analyze what was going on. Time was ticking by rapidly, and the sun was setting at the horizon. Although Jay had been very busy observing this young lady, he hadn't cared to observe the landscape or the roads he took while following her.

He wanted Mack, especially since he realized this could not be his Sasha. He wanted to go near the dock but was lost. He looked around desperately but there was no one in sight. Helpless, he walked toward their cottage and overheard loud voices arguing. At first, he felt disconcerted to bother them, but he had no choice, so he knocked. He got no response as the voices were still busy arguing. This time he knocked harder which was followed by silence. Then he heard heavy footsteps coming toward the door. He quickly took a few steps backward and waited. The door came ajar.

"What?" this man shouted.

"Hi, my name is Jay. I am new to the island. I have lost my way. Can you guide me to the docks?" he said with a forced smile while keeping his heartbeats in check.

Ray scratched his head and looked around with a frown. He called out to Maya, who was already very irritated with him but became curious when Ray mentioned someone had lost his way and needed help.

She walked out with the toddler in her arms and was surprised to see Jay. Her first reaction was, "You?"

He got flustered, blushing hard and trying not to say anything.

"Do you know him?" was Ray's first reaction. She was quick to deny and then clarified that he was one of her customers and bought a lot of her food.

Obliged, Ray greeted him with a smile that showed off his dark, stained teeth to which Jay scrunched his nose.

"I can show you the way back to the docks." Ray was quick to offer, but seeing Jay's crumpled-up nose, Maya quickly put on her sandals and walked out with her toddler in her arms.

"Don't worry. I will show him the way and pick up some fish on my way back. You boil some rice in the meantime," she ordered and started walking with steady steps. Jay had to run after her as she was very brisk.

"Hi, I'm Jay," he introduced himself to which she gave a 'whatever' with her body language.

"Wait up," he pleaded. She did not care to do so.

Finally, he caught up with her, and after catching a breath or two, he came to the point, "So, you are not Sasha?"

"Who is Sasha?" she asked with a frown and a brief pause in her walk.

"Sasha is my girlfriend," he said, then quickly nodded his head. "Was my girlfriend."

She continued to wear that frown while walking at the same speed.

"You resemble her. Except that she does not have a husband and a baby." She twisted her lips this time as if to curse him. He tried hard to ignore it although those lips reminded him of her, again.

There was a pause, then she said in a cold tone, "She *was* your girlfriend. How do you know she does *not* have a husband and a baby, *now*?" she sneered at him. He got cold feet and reduced his speed and was left behind.

"Walk fast. I don't have all day!" she shouted to which he came out of his reverie and sped toward her.

"There is the dock." She pointed in a certain direction. He wanted to say thanks, but she walked away without saying goodbye. He felt sad, but when he saw Mack from a distance, he walked quickly toward him like a baby runs toward his parents.

"Where were you?" Mack inquired in an earnest tone. "I got so worried."

"I drifted away deep into the island as I was following a lady thinking her to be Sasha," Jay said in a childlike tone.

Mack got curious. "Who's Sasha?"

Two tents were pitched, and the two tribal people were already in one of them. Jay could hear their snores, and upon hearing Mack's query, he gave out a cold sigh as he sat down on the sand next to the empty tent with both his hands on his legs. "Sasha was my life, and she was everything to me. Until she deserted me... left me alone and dry." He let out a sigh and eyed Mack whose eyebrows were raised as if he wanted more.

"I acquired my Masters in Commerce and secretly applied for an MBA in the United States. Little did I know that I would get accepted. Once the letter of admission came in from Santa Clara University, my mom and grandparents openly showed their disappointment. I had agreed to major in a field that would help to continue to expand the business set up by my granddad, which was nurtured by my dad and now my mom. I waved goodbye to my homeland and started my journey in a new country.

I accidentally bumped into Sasha at a coffee shop even before my first class, and then the relationship between us just continued to deepen. Her outgoing and outspoken temperament complemented my personality, making me forget all about my past. My bruises healed in her presence since she was always peppy about every darn thing. I vividly remember the day when I had asked her to move in with me, and her first reaction was, "Phew, it's high time. I thought you would never ask." This memory made Jay laugh his heart out, and with moist eyes, he continued. "She was such a genuine person. She always spoke her heart, although there were moments when it would scare me to the core since the relationship was going faster than a lightning McQueen."

"Who is that?" Mack inquired, confused.

Jay stared back at him and realized what part of the world he lived in, so he just nodded his head. "Never mind. Soon we graduated. She was a people person, so she chose a field in marketing while I chose to specialize in innovation and entrepreneurship as I had promised to go back to my country and help out."

There was a pause, and then he continued with a soft chuckle. "When she agreed to move in with me, those were the best months of my life. Gosh, she just loved to live life and made me an addict, too! We both got a job in different companies, so we worked hard during the day and partied crazy at night," he said with dreamy eyes, to which Mack was quick to interrupt.

"How can you party crazy?" he asked with a sneer.

"Well, she loved drinking booze and could not control herself as shots after shots were quenched like a thirsty bird. I was always happy to be her partner in crime." His eyes beamed as he continued, "We danced on tabletops after those shots and got kicked out of the bar. There was a time we even maxed out my credit card." He chuckled. "I cannot even imagine doing that now."

There was silence. Jay was unperturbed, he was having a blast by reminiscing the past, and there were no inhibitions as he went on and on. "Sasha was such a cracker that she would even go streaking graffiti on the walls at night. But, she was an artist. I called it art." He grinned, then put his hand over his mouth.

"You know we even went skinny dipping in my colleague's pool once." He flashed his pearly whites and continued. "We were supposed to go feed his birds and water the many plants his wife had while they were away vacationing in a different country."

He stayed in that moment for long, then with dreamy eyes carried on. "We had an exceptional intimate bond, and that's what made this relationship so special. I took it to the next level by proposing to her on the night when we broke the law."

"You guys broke the law?"

"I know. She was able to make me do any darn thing." He chuckled loudly, slightly embarrassed but did not deter in exposing himself. "We were drunk, and she challenged me to follow a taxi that was speeding since it had a woman in labor inside the vehicle. Result... the cop asked us to stop and issued me a ticket. I not only had to pay the fine but also attend traffic school. My insurance spiked up causing more debt. Boy, it was something I had never imagined. My adrenaline was at an all-time high with her."

Mack, in his heart of hearts, thought, *Phew, she was a bomb in disguise. Glad they broke up.*

Soon, Jay's mood changed. He became quiet with a sulking face. "Things changed when she lost her job. She was home while I worked. Now with one paycheck, we could not afford the same lifestyle. I tried to hold her back. She resisted. There were fights, arguments, and not talking to each other for days. Our relationship was hurting, and I avoided going home until midnight just to avoid any more verbal fights."

He paused, but Mack was quick to respond, "Was this your first ever relationship?"

"Yes, I have been very hurt since then," he said in a sullen tone, touching his heart. "My heart still aches," he said in a boyish tone.

Mack felt like shouting at him to grow up, but instead just nodded with a smirk. "You will get over it. In fact, whatever happens, happens for a reason. Were you able to pay off your credit card debts?" He changed the topic.

"Yes, I did. Money became my dear friend as I saved every penny. My mom had paid for my post-graduation tuition, so when I got into debt, it made me feel so heavy at heart. And to top it off, Sasha left me."

Jay was brooding, and Mack was quick to come to terms. "Grow up! Hearing what she was like, it was a blessing in disguise," he said, which came as a shock to the tea man who stared at him in confusion.

Then after a pause, Jay confessed in a sincere tone, "I never had so much fun in my life as when Sasha was around."

"Fun?" Mack chuckled. "You have not tasted fun, my friend. Alcohol deludes the mind and the laughter is entertaining, but did you realize what the end product was..." he let out a sigh, "... debts and heartbreak?"

Jay was not convinced. Then Mack queried from another angle, "So none of your friends ever advised you to end this relationship?"

Jay stared at him for a bit, and then with a lump in his throat, he said in an unreserved tone, "Actually, all my friends loved partying as we did." After a pause, he shrugged his shoulder. "I guess we all were on the wrong boat!" Jay pondered over his statement as he said in a soft voice and chose to go lie down in the tent. Mack took a second glance to both his boats anchored and covered well. He snickered at them and called it a night as well.

Morning came at the crack of dawn as there was an echo of a mixed group of birds. Jay woke up with a start, but Mack was quick to define each noise as the gull, the ducks, the geese, the pelicans, and the herons as they all had a distinctive sound. Having lived on this island for years, he was never wrong.

They freshened up in the nearby restroom and unloaded their boats on two carts with wheels that were rented courtesy of the barter system. An aroma pulled Jay in a certain direction as he walked like a miffed monkey toward it. Mack moved his head from one side to the other thinking this guy is sheer trouble.

Soon, Jay walked with a recycled container that had four cups in its holder. He offered the cups to the three men who had many questions to which he just kept a steady, smiling face and had a standard response, "Try it!"

Soon, the three sat on the ground and were relishing the warm drink while Jay was also doing the same but would eye them now and then.

"I remember tasting this when I was living with my relatives," Mack said as he would blow it occasionally and sip it gently while the other two were savoring it.

"This is my occupation," said a proud Jay and went on to clarify, "I have a tea café back home." The word home made him pause for a bit, and then he went on. "I serve tea with all sorts of condiments in it," he said with a smile that had a lot of pride.

"Yes, I remember you mentioning it," Mack said.

"Mack, can we buy some loose tea from here? I can offer everyone at the island my specialty," he inquired with glee. Mack inquired from his tribal brethren, and they were nodding in a frenzy. Jay was very enthusiastic about it and started blabbering about the menu at his café to which Mack would occasionally nod while they were pushing the carts of produce toward a busy bazaar.

The sales were phenomenal as the goods were being sold amazingly fast for two main reasons—first, the pricing was extremely below the market price, and second, the quality was far beyond any other vendor. Jay would get glimpses of the twin Sasha selling her home-cooked food in a stall a few feet away from their carts. For lunch, he purchased food for his *fellas* from her, which gave him another chance to mingle with her. She was at first quite irritated seeing him, but toward sunset, the duo had socialized quite a bit where he got a peek into her life, her toddler, and her lazy husband who happened to be her childhood sweetheart.

*Life is not fair! She is such a diligent, sincere, and whole-hearted person. What does she get in return?* Jay mumbled, cleaning the cart while Mack and his tribal brethren counted the earnings. The four walked toward Mack's relatives' house where they chose to spend the night after a warm home-cooked meal in an actual warm bed with cotton sheets, a comforter, and a pillow made of cotton fabric instead of the wood that he used for his head at the island. Jay was aware of everything around him, grateful and appreciative of the food, the tea, the warm water chugging from the pipes, and he was looking forward to some new clothes which he and Mack were going to buy the next day.

The other two tribal men sailed off with one boat while Mack and Jay had another night to shop.

"Hey, Jay! Tomorrow before we get all the supplies for our family back at the island, let's go have some fun," Mack said in an earnest tone.

"Fun without alcohol?" Jay mumbled to himself with raised eyebrows.

Morning came at the usual hour. A warm bath, a hearty breakfast of pancakes, poached eggs, sausage, and cereal with milk—the usual food he had at home which brought back warm memories. Mack was eyeing him as he would relish and comment on each morsel that would usually be about his memories of back home.

"You miss home, my friend!" Mack could not resist. "You deny it, but your heart takes you there," he said with a smirk. "Don't forget to call home and inform them about your welfare."

Jay sneered in return and chose to eat the rest of his food in silence.

Soon, they headed giving Jay the jitters—the actual meaning of what fun is without making him lightheaded. While walking, they saw many red candy canes, moss wreaths on the front of each entryway, and lights, reindeer, and inflated snowman.

Jay skipped a heartbeat. "What? Is it Christmas yet? Did I miss Thanksgiving?"

Mack shrugged his shoulder. "For me, every day is Christmas and Thanksgiving!" He chuckled then casually peeked at a newsstand looking out for the date.

"Christmas is in twenty days."

"That's my favorite holiday," Jay said with wide eyes. "On Christmas Day at my café, I ask my friend, Sam, to disguise as Santa, and wow, what a magnificent turnaround I get even on that day. Business booms even on that day!" He chuckled with pride.

The word 'business' made Mack nod his head without any emotion. They reached a place with many rides. Jay scrunched his nose at that sight.

"What's wrong?" asked Mack

"These are for kids."

"Who said that? Who labeled it?"

Jay pondered over that statement, then shrugged his shoulders and walked along. At first hesitant, he then sat in the Ferris wheel cage. As the wheel spun upward with the help of gears and motors, gravity pulled the wheel back down again. This continuous cycle was the ride which gradually increased in speed, giving Jay tickles in his stomach. At first, he resisted by changing his posture while holding the bar with a strong grip to avoid showing his excitement, but then he eventually couldn't hold it any longer. He chuckled at first with inhibition, then he let go. Letting go made him feel liberated as his laughter was loud and energetic. He was now expressing it via words like 'Whoa' and 'Ooo' as the ride continued. He was in a world of his own as he was howling and rejoicing at every move of the wheel even though the average speed was ten miles per hour, but his emotions were twirling at a much faster rate. Mack was placed above him in the ride and loved the fact that Jay had loosened up. Gradually, the speed reduced, and every rider was escorted out of his seat. When it was Jay's turn, he resisted for a bit. Then his eyes met Mack who could understand his feelings. "Want another turn?" he inquired to which Jay was quick to nod yes.

"Okay, let's do it."

They took another ride, and this time Jay's voice was piercing. He felt embarrassed when the ride stopped, and onlookers were staring at him. This time he did not take a second to get down. But when with Mack, he did not have to say a word—his facial expressions said it all. The wrinkles around his eyes and lips seemed to have disappeared. His eyes were dilated due to the excitement, and his face was red due to the rush of blood.

"Can we go on that ride?" Jay was quick to point at the merry-go-round.

"You want to sit on fake horses? Children sit on them," Mack was quick to add, but Jay was unperturbed. The fun bug was in him, and nothing could deter him.

Being morning, there was not much of a line, so they were seated on the pony of their choice. Jay was very excited as he held on the neck of the pony while looking around with an amused look.

"Hold on, everybody, the ride is starting," came an announcement, and the platform slowly turned round and round with each animal gliding up and down a pole. At first, Jay's eyes widened while he continued to cling to his pony. Then, he shrieked and howled and snickered. His expressions were childlike as he enjoyed the ride that was also giving him a blast from the past. He recollected how he would go with his dad to their local fair, and the background of shrieks and laughter were still the same. He chuckled over it with moist eyes as if time had frozen.

Once he got off the ride, he did not hesitate to share his feelings with Mack. After relishing a cotton candy, they were off to the market to purchase the goods for all the people on the island, which Mack called home and Jay had fond sentiments of.

Jay was super excited to buy basic clothing for himself. Little did he realize that a pair of pants and shirt were just mere clothing. He did not care for brand names or color combinations. All he wanted was basic clothing for survival. He felt so fulfilled over the thought.

He never felt such intent pleasure as he did when they were shopping for the folks and the little infant. His heart was flowing with love and compassion. He had a high state of excitement, and he was a riot of emotions as they were peaking and crashing within him like the waves in the ocean. He realized how much interest Mack was taking in him, and he too would try to do the same. The thrill for caring and purchasing according to their needs was giving him so much pleasure within that he could feel his heart melt, and the smile he was wearing was without any inhibitions.

Amongst all these purchases, he would now and then experience a bad taste in his mouth courtesy of the money. When Mack would pay them after a certain amount, some shopkeepers would be finicky about exact change. But the big heart of Mack would churn everything sour into sweet by giving them more than what they asked for, leaving their mouths wide open, baffled, and puzzled. Some of them would get embarrassed and refuse to take extra while a handful of them would slyly take it unnoticed.

Jay realized how the transactions would change his mood and even pondered over the different temperaments of the people on the island. That included Maya's too, who had her baby today since her husband had gone job hunting. She would be very particular to take payment before serving food. A big bowl on her stall asking for tips with a mantra that was at first very amusing to him, 'Tips can change Karma' reminded him of his café. He chuckled at first and then was embarrassed over it.

While enjoying some local food, Mack reminded him again of contacting his folks at home. Jay looked around for a payphone, and when he could not find it, he inquired from Maya, who shrugged her shoulders at first, then offered her cell phone.

"Err... it could be an international call, but I will pay you for it," he declared before dialing to which she was quick to extend her hand for the money. He grinned at first, then placed a twenty-dollar bill in her palm.

Jay knew Gina's number and said it out loud while she dialed it with her baby in one arm. It went to voice mail. She handed the phone to him to which he muttered something and hung up.

Mack, on the other side, was making sure he had bought for all, and Jay, after hanging up, noticed Mack had bundles of extra cash and was curious what he would do with it. "Nothing! I will give it to my uncle here. He can use it for whatever he likes," he said in a detached tone.

Jay fumbled at first, then quickly thought about the conversation he had earlier and inquired, "Could we buy some tea leaves? I would like to entice the members on the island with my tea skills."

"Thanks for reminding me, Jay." Mack liked the idea, and the duo went shopping.

Evening came quickly, and the duo headed to Mack's relatives' home. They went to bed early since they were going to board their boat to Mack's home in the morning.

# CHAPTER TWENTY-SIX

*"You don't always get the treasure by holding on. Sometimes the magic happens*
*when you let go." —* <u>*Leylah Attar*</u>

Back home, Gina's grandparents and aunt arrived at Jay's. Sam secretly went to pick them up from the airport with the pretext that his friend's relatives were arriving. When the four arrived at the café, it was busy with a long line waiting to order. They could see Gina at a distance taking orders vigilantly and executing each order one by one. The gloomy aunt with short white hair, a height of five-feet-two inches and a petite frame with her in-laws stood in the line to order a beverage for themselves. The father-in-law even though he was using a cane to support his arthritic legs, had a personality along with his bushy mustache and gold-rimmed glasses that he wore over his olive skin. The mother-in-law had a bun of peppered hair adorned with a scarf given the cold weather of December. When their turn came to order, it surprised Gina. She gave out a loud cry. The four hugged and cried bringing everything to a standstill.

Sam took over the reins of taking and making the orders while all four of them sat in one corner and talked about the one person in their lives who had taken their spirit of life with him as he was 'missing' in action. Usha had bandaged her emotional wounds with valor and took over the business since the aging grandparents were still rickety about their son's decision to go to the mountains. Gina and Jay, the teens, were Usha's inspiration as she continued her life with the nine-to-seven job of the never-ending rat race. Her grit and determination to learn gave the company deserved success and recognition in India. Unfortunately, both the children chose to go abroad for further studies, but Usha was patient and compassionate enough to let them live their lives with the hope they would come back. Alas, little did she know that fate had other plans? Her once big, wide eyes had dark circles and had sunk in as if they were mere sockets in her skull. Wrinkles were plenty on her forehead that even without raising her eyebrows, they could be seen as distinct lines. But she kept her poise while listening to all the details from Gina, continuing to sip her son's tea. Feeling honored to be sitting in his café, her maternal instincts were proud of his achievements, but she was still not coming to terms with his going away. Her heart kept denying while her brain was trying to concentrate on the latest updates from her niece. The grandparents were too old to accept another loss, so they just stared at Gina.

Just then, there was that same peculiar knock on the glass window. Gina got up immediately to get the order while Usha looked in that direction. After focusing hard, she cried out loud, "Chandrika?"

"Is that you, Chandrika?" she got up and walked in that direction.

Gina was shocked at first, then immediately caught her aunt's elbow and corrected her, but Usha just nodded her head in dismay. With moist eyes, she let go of her elbow and walked out of the café toward her with a face that had excitement and surprise written all over it.

This lady in mask was in the middle of folding her umbrella, but when she heard the name '*Chandrika,*' she was appalled. Her eyes were wide open as she looked around letting out a sigh that was loud and intense. She looked in the direction of the voice and was even more startled. Her knees gave way, and she lost her balance while trying to reach out to this voice. Fortunately, Usha was quick to hold her hand and help her stand back on her feet.

"When did you get here?" was Cee-Cee aka Chandrika's query. Usha updated her about Sam's call and the surprise visit to Gina.

"I am so sorry about Jay!" said Cee-Cee in an impassioned tone while continuing to hold Usha's arm.

In the café, Gina was aghast seeing how the two women were interacting outside. With the beverage cup in her hand and a brown bag, she continued to glare. *How can this be? Usha auntie's sister, Chandrika, had succumbed in that fire! That's what Jay told me. Did she survive? Why did Jay keep this secret from me?*

She felt betrayed and went to inquire from her grandparents who were equally surprised by her presence as they were also looking out at the two women. Gina needed answers, so with the beverage cup and the brown bag, she walked with ginger steps toward them. Usha wiped her tears and looked in her direction.

"Hello, Chandrika auntie! Or should I still call you Cee-Cee? Gosh, I am so confused. Why did you keep this from me?" Gina came to the point since her heart was aching, and she felt cheated, especially since she took extra care of her when Jay left for his vacation.

Cee-Cee stretched her hand in her direction while patting her shoulder. "I had asked Jay to keep this as our little secret. Even Usha, my sister, was not aware that I am breathing," she said in an impartial tone. "Look at me. I am all burned, which is why I cover myself from top to bottom while just allowing my eyes and mouth to be visible. Even for that, I have to use an umbrella to avoid the sun's rays from torturing my skin. Nothing's the same since that fire broke out in my house where Jay was the tenant as an MBA student."

Usha interjected, "You could have informed me about you surviving, sister! You know I cried and cried until the tears refused to come," she said in an annoyed tone.

"I had to find my life, Usha. After I made sure Jay was settled with Sasha as those two were cozy with each other, I went away in search of my own goals while making Jay promise not to tell anyone about my survival. I needed this time to find what to do next. My current situation inspired me to help other burn victims, encouraging me to open an NGO. I could not rely on you or anybody for that matter. You, of all, should be able to understand," she said with a passionate tone and teary eyes.

"So, what do you do now?" Usha came to the point as if forgetting all about the past. "What's keeping you busy?"

"Well, my nonprofit to assist burn victims has received an overwhelming response, allowing me to continue with this venture. My focus is on assisting the survivors of burns and burn-related injuries to learn to live with their scars. I, with the help of other organizations, get projects for them to be able to survive financially. Once I came back to this town, I got in touch with Jay. I was very sorry to hear about his fling with Sasha and was literally with him in spirit when he transitioned from his corporate job to opening this café. I would swing by once a day after my work to grab his signature beverage and a snack."

By this time, the grandparents walked toward her and everyone met with teary eyes. The old couple complimented her commendable valor.

"Truly hats off to both of you for your boldness to tackle any challenges that come into your lives!" Gina's granddad said in a laudatory tone to which the two women giggled like schoolgirls, but Gina was quick to bring them out of that mood, "We have another challenge to overcome, though! There is no news from Jay yet."

All were solemn over it, but the grandma was quick to break the silence. In a voice that was shaky, she said with confidence, "He is alive and walking miles emotionally. Let's give him time. He will come back."

"Amen!" All were quick to say that in unison.

"Why don't you and Usha auntie bond at Jay's apartment?" Gina handed the keys to Usha while signaling Sam to take them all to freshen up.

"I can drive," Cee-Cee defended herself. "I will meet you at his abode."

When everyone went in their own direction, Gina felt confident to face this situation, especially after her grandma's benediction. She went into the café to resume her orders when she saw a missed call and a voicemail from an unknown number. She crossed her eyebrows for a bit and then got back to her business since all she could think of was the cruise line. She would get plenty of unknown calls thanks to the many random callers calling to either ask for subscriptions to newspapers or home insurance or just to change phone carriers. *Blah!*

When Sam came back, she took a breather and chose to sit with her phone. Reluctantly, she clicked on her voicemail to hear the message. At first, she heard a baby crying, then it was followed by a lady's voice trying to shush the baby. Gina lost it and was about to hang up when she heard a familiar voice, a voice that she was yearning to hear. A sound that gave her the rush as her heartbeats got faster, and with that came a gush of tears. Her actions were senseless as she at first stared at the phone then played it again. This time she put it on speaker so that she did not miss anything. But the voice she was yearning to hear was just for a microsecond as the baby's cry overpowered everything.

She quickly dialed the number, but it was going to voicemail. Desperate, she went to Sam who, on seeing her physical and emotional state, was shocked at first. After listening to the voicemail a couple of times, he made a conclusion that was not in favor of Gina. This made her blood boil with anger as she cursed herself for starting to get delusional. She felt her idle mind needed to get busy, so she went about the usual chores and put in her earbuds, turning on some music that was deafening her since even Sam could hear it from a distance. He felt sorry for her but also glad that her relatives were here so they could all grieve and heal together.

The music continued even after an hour. He tapped on her shoulder to get her attention. She looked up with a raised eyebrow. Once she lowered the volume, Sam said, "Why don't you go home early? I will clean up after the evening class and lock up!"

After a bit of contemplation exhibited by biting her lips, she agreed and drove off. She had tears in her eyes as her mind was recapping all those incidents when Jay would shield her as a brother or simply hold her hand when she would have a crisis. After parking her car in the parking lot, she listened the voicemail again. And this time, she felt the man's voice was nowhere close to Jay. Cursing herself

again, she half-heartedly dialed the number.
	The person at the other end picked up the phone!

# CHAPTER TWENTY-SEVEN

*"Life is about experience... You can't hold on to everything."* —
*Sarah Addison Allen*

Jay and Mack navigated their boats after loading their goods and started their journey back home. Jay was very excited with his new clothes, razor, and loose tea. He was looking forward to brewing tea and serving them with different condiments each day. The return trip seemed shorter since there was excitement in the air for both the young adults until they saw a peculiar boat on their shores that made Mack's heart skip a beat. He looked through his telescope to double confirm, and he was afraid that what he saw was true. The flag on that boat said it all. He was mumbling, and Jay was the silent listener while gulping now and then.

"Now that the pirates have invaded the island, what do we do?" Jay inquired in a gullible tone. Mack was equally confused and had no response. He was only thinking of his people and their reaction, hoping that they all were unharmed. "They can be our guests since we have ample produce to feed many mouths," was Mack's response, which took Jay by surprise as he just stared at him.

The sun was above them indicating it was noon. They hit the barren shore and slowly walked toward the huts. All they could hear were unfamiliar voices shouting and laughing. Mack walked with steady steps. His heart was beating rapidly, but he did not show it on his face. He walked with a strutted chest and head held high and stopped at those voices. After a deep inhalation, he greeted in a gentle tone.

"Ahoy to you!" said a man whose one eye was patched up. He smiled showing off his tobacco-stained teeth that made Jay twitch his nose while Mack continued to stare at him. "How can my island help you?" He came to the point.

"Ahoy! My people call me Tiger Lily." He extended his hand covered in a white glove. The glove was taintless white while the man was stinky and covered with mud. That confused Mack and Jay, but they kept their cool.

"I'm amazed at how self-sufficient your island is. Your yields are so good that you all eat, live, and never complain. Sadly, I came here for treasures, and I don't find any. Although I don't trust your men, and my men are digging around to find it." Then he glanced at their boat using a telescope, "Do you have it on that boat of yours?" he said, pointing at the recent boat they undocked.

Jay gulped. Mack pretended not to hear it and stood there with a stern face while Tiger Lilly ordered his men to get the goods from that boat. When the goods were laid on the ground, they were amazed at the clothing, the few essential things, and the big bag of tea.

"This has a strong aroma. What do you plan on doing with this?" the captain inquired while sniffing at the bag of tea.

Jay stepped in, "I make delicious tea."

"Make some for us," he ordered.

Jay got down to business while Mack surveyed the island and talked discreetly to his tribe. He was relieved to know that no one was hurt, although his heart was hurting seeing random digs from the pirates searching for hidden treasure. *"Why are they so surprised that man can live without treasures?"* he muttered to himself since amidst their random digging, they uprooted many plants, and that's what made his heart flutter.

Thanks to the condiments growing plentiful on the island, Jay splurged over the mint and cardamom as he made two batches of tea. He added agave as a sweetener and offered the tea to everyone. Surprisingly, they enjoyed it, especially since the sun had set, and the clouds had come in dropping the temperature to a cool sixty-five degrees Fahrenheit.

Jay was basking in the compliments from the tribal men while the handful of pirates were a little confused. Usually, sunset meant they opened up their toddy bottles, but since their chief commanded them to sip the hot beverage, they were drinking it obediently.

"So, tell me once again how you guys survive?" asked Tiger Lilly as he held the wooden cup in his gloved hand and brushed his long unkempt hair with the other hand.

"What you see is what we have. We eat what we grow. We survive from it," Mack was downright honest in his response, but the chief could still not digest the fact. He then inquired from his men which part of the island was left to be surveyed, and they pointed in a particular direction.

"I may take your word since we have been here for one night and no luck so far. Honestly, besides the food, and now this tea," he eyed Jay, "I don't find anything attractive on this island of yours," he said in a very honest tone which made Mack chuckle but Jay nervous since destiny had always played in a very unusual manner for him. He was scared that the pirates don't kidnap him for making tea for them.

"This tea-making is so simple. You just boil the leaves in hot water and brew them with various condiments," Jay tried to clarify so that he is out of their zone. He eyed all the pirates while describing the art of tea-making. The chief was the only one who listened intently while the others were either too tired or just waiting for the fish to be grilled so they could open their bottles and call it a night.

Dinner was a chaotic affair. The tribal folk kept their cool and served their guests prior to eating themselves. Soon, these freeloaders were a merry lot as the alcohol had seeped into their system, and they were either laughing or dancing away to music that was humming in their brains. Jay observed them and recapped his life when he and Sasha were like them. He felt foolish and a nincompoop. *What was I thinking? Glad Sasha is out of my life,* he thought as he helped the tribal people clean up.

The booze had got into their system to such an extent that they slept with a fire basking while the others retreated to their shelters. It was a long day for Jay, and after seeing the 'fun aspect' of life, he did not complain about sleeping on the hard surface. Sleep came quickly since his body and mind were exhausted.

Morning was at the usual hour thanks to the farm animals while the buccaneers were still snoring. He freshened up and got to his favorite chore of making tea and enjoyed passing the cups to all who savored it along with their breakfast. The tribal folk got to work in the fields while the pirates continued to uproot and create havoc by their loud outcries of not being able to find anything.

Two more nights went by, and Tiger Lilly was getting restless since riches and abundance was not in sight. All he could feel was the tranquility and wisdom of these tribal people in this so-called fantasy island that was self-sufficient in its own way. It irked him to see how these people were committed to preserving their tradition of fauna and flora and were okay living along with it. At first, he found them hopeless and aimless people, but soon the serenity in the aurora caught him as he started to observe the innocence yet the strength and courage these people endowed as they worked hard the whole day tilling the land so they could have bags of produce.

The little infant's red cheeks and eyes sparkling with mirth and fire made him the attraction as all took turns to play with him. The chief was worried that he and his team would lose their identity if they lived amongst these peace-loving people for long. They kept with that regime so that these pirates didn't become one like them. They loaded their boat with bags of grains and even took a few pounds of tea on the boat. Then one fine day, Tiger Lilly announced, "I hate to say this, but I am tired of living on this island that is not only spectacular but is threatening our cult. If we continue to live here, we will change, and I cannot afford to lose my cult over it," he said in a very serious tone, but it made Jay and Mack giggle like crazy. When the tribal people looked on with curiosity, Mack interpreted. There was an outburst of laughter that made the pirates very confused at first, and then with embarrassment, they said their goodbyes and sailed away.

The tribal folk went about their business since even while these buccaneers were here, they did not feel threatened. Their life had to go back to normal for them, even with their absence.

# CHAPTER TWENTY-EIGHT

*"We cannot hold a torch to light another's path without brightening our own."*
— *Ben Sweetland*

"Hello, uhh... I got a call from this number where a man was trying to leave me a message."

"Huh?" Gina got a confused response.

"Hello... umm, could I speak to Jay?" Gina came to the point.

That was followed by silence.

Gina felt foolish. *Sam was correct. That did not sound like Jay.* She was about to hang up when the lady responded, "He is not here. He left for his island."

"What?" Gina was practically shouting on the phone, "Jay is alive?"

"Huh?" the above response got Maya confused.

"Which island? Where did he go?" Gina continued to talk in a high-pitched tone on the phone, and soon she realized that it was not helping since, on the other end, there was only silence. That made Jay's cousin take a couple of deep breaths, and then she said in a very calm tone, "My cousin, Jay, went missing due to a shipwreck. I want to know which island he is on. I can ask the cruise line to go look for him."

"I don't know," was Maya's response.

Gina was getting restless, but she wanted some answers rather than hitting a blank wall, so she continued, "What is the name of your island?"

That's when Maya got defensive. "Why?" she asked.

Gina replayed the whole story again. She tried to play the emotional card, which made Maya finally give away the name of her island, "Tora-Tora."

Gina found the name very unusual. She made a mental note of it and hung up. At first, she just stared at the steering wheel. Then she stared at the phone. She got so confused for a bit that Gina had no idea how to react. A cousin who had gone missing for over a month is found. She cried and laughed at the same time while thanking the Lord, and amidst all this, her head hit the steering wheel when the horn went off. She got a shock and shrieked. That was followed by a pause, and then she cried again. This time a car pulled next to her. It was her neighbor. Seeing her in that state, he inquired about her welfare to which she was quick to pull down her window and narrate the whole episode. He was least interested but showed his two thumbs up and went his way. Now the news of Jay being alive sunk in. She quickly got out of the car and walked toward Jay's townhome.

Since she had the key, she barged right in shouting, "Jay is alive! Jay is alive!"

The grandparents were sleeping in her room while his mom was lying down in Jay's bedroom. She walked out with hurried steps, "Shhh... your grandparents just went to sleep. Please don't disturb them."

Gina continued to talk in a loud decibel. "Grandma was correct. Jay is alive."

Usha's eyes filled with tears as she crossed her hands. "I hope you are correct, Gina," she said in a subdued tone.

"Yes, I have evidence. I just spoke to a lady on the island of Tora-Tora." That confused Usha, then Gina was quick to play the voice mail on her phone's speaker asking her to listen carefully, and voila! A mom would know better than anybody when it comes to her child's voice. She recognized it instantly. She became frantic and shrieked with joy while tears rolled down her cheeks. Granddad heard all the commotion and eventually he and grandma were updated about Jay's survival.

After rejoicing with them for a good hour or two, she called the cruise line and briefed them about the island while asking them to look for him in the nearby islands. Usha was quick to update her sister, Cee-Cee a.k.a. Chandrika. That evening was not quiet since the four of them were busy either taking a walk down memory lane and bursting into tears or calling up family and friends in India to update them about Jay.

# CHAPTER TWENTY-NINE

*"Everything is held together with stories. That is all that is holding us together,*
*stories and compassion." — <u>Barry López</u>*

Days were rolling into weeks. Jay had never felt so at peace by facing the demons of his past. The frequent nightmares he used to have were no more ever since he had encrypted the voice to be his mom. His heart had healed after realizing that Sasha was a mistake, and it was a blessing that they had broken up. However, his dad was constantly in his mind courtesy of baby Anil who was named after him and was getting naughtier day by day. He had many questions for his dad and wondered if he should let it all go or maybe just visit him to check on his welfare. There were days he would think of him when splashing water from a bucket or sleeping on the hard surface with a wooden plank as a pillow. *Would his life be as simple as this?* he wondered as he would sweat in the sun ploughing and sowing seeds that will eventually turn into a bountiful harvest in a couple of months for them to enjoy.

He even noticed how his muscles had shaped around his arms and calves. Once a gangly, tall man, he was now a barrel-chested, brawny man easily comparable to the Brawny Paper Towel man who would clean any tough mess that life would throw at him. His ability and agility had doubled in the last few months. And now, he actually thanked his stars for landing on an island that made him mentally strong, allowing his cough that was rattling his chest to die down.

Jay's attitude of working quietly in the fields and being content with himself made Mack initiate the question, "When do you plan on going home?" he asked in a direct tone.

Jay was stunned at first, then after a pause, "You don't want me here anymore?" he inquired in an amused tone. Mack mocked at his query and kept quiet.

Jay continued, "Actually, I want to go home since I miss my mom and also want to meet my dad to check on his welfare. Maybe even compare notes with him. I have lived this lifestyle of detachment, and I want to see if he, too, has that halo above his head like all of you here possess."

Mack gave a very steady smile. "I can make arrangements for you to leave."

"Tomorrow morning, let's sail to that island, and you can contact your cruise line from there. They will make arrangements to take you home."

There were mixed feelings for Jay. He felt excited but also sad. That night, he was confused about what to pack and what to leave behind since nothing was his and yet everything belonged to him. The memories he wrapped them well, but when it came to personal belongings, he realized he had none, yet felt so liberated from his heart. The jacket that he would wear all the time since it had a pocket where his cash was stashed was deliberately left on Tora-Tora after he saw Mack leaving all the extra-unused cash with his relatives. The clothing he was wearing was enough for him to sustain until he reached his home in California.

"You should meet Yogi and inform him of you two leaving tomorrow morning," Mack said in an insistent tone. For a bit, Jay was confused since he was wondering why Yogi needs time. He can just leave with him that very morning, but little did he realize how attached his canine had become to the other farm animals. When Jay mentioned to him about their leaving this island, Yogi gave off a loud whine followed by constant woofs that he had to be consoled by the farm master while Jay looked upon them with a confused look.

The next morning was a very emotional sight since not only did the thirty humans lineup but also some farm animals were there to say their final adios to their Yogi. While the humans chose to hug and show their gratitude, Yogi chose to sniff the backsides of the pets. It was amazing how the cows, cats, sheep, goats, geese, and dogs mingled in no time. Their shapes and sizes had nothing to do with the emotions they exhibited.

Ahe said something which made Mack chuckle. Jay looked at him with curiosity to which Mack clarified, "My dad is saying that they will remember you through the tea they all have become addicted to."

Jay was flattered and bowed. Soon the duo was on a boat with Mack and another tribal man for company. Jay breathed deeply as he allowed the wind to blow his long tresses, which he chose to grow while continuing to shave off his facial hair. He stared at the shore and serene surroundings since he was sure such vibes would never be inhaled or seen anywhere else on this planet. The people and their unique characteristics toward life not only added an exclusive dimension to this island but also allowed them to live a life filled with love, yet they were detached with everything that included materialism and even humans.

He, for once, thanked his destiny for the chain of events that occurred allowing him to land in a zone where even the evil-minded pirates could not sustain for long. This island and the people not only changed his physical appearance thanks to the slogging in the fields but also unlocked his mindset of Sasha and his parents. He was able to break the shackles of the past that were inhibiting him from walking a single step in the present toward a future he had always dreamed of but never dared to step on that path.

He felt he could breathe better courtesy of Mack and the island that helped cure the tickle in his throat. Courtesy of this lifestyle, he experienced no stress, no negativity, and was amazed at how it affected his mind. He was interested to know more about his dad, who had now been living away from civilization for over a decade. He was curious how it would have changed him since he felt a bud blossom within him in just a few weeks' time.

With moist eyes, he waved to them all, and at this moment, he really wished he had his phone to click pictures of them all, but instead chose to absorb it all in his neurons and continued staring hard. He was mindful of everything around him. The sail toward Tora-Tora was a quiet affair since Jay was reliving all the possible moments with a constant smile on his face, which depicted contentment. However, there was a certain heaviness in his heart to which he would frown now and then to dissect, but either Yogi's tactics or Mack's words would distract him.

Time was ticking, and this yearning in his heart was making him very anxious to which he frowned upon and concentrated by seating himself toward the end of the boat while overlooking the ocean to avoid any distractions. Mack observed this and gave him the space to do so.

Jay realized it was his dad. Somewhere within his subconscious mind, he still wanted to connect with him, wanted to peek into his life and get a visual of him in the present state. Unknowingly, a tear trickled down as he realized that it's not possible since his dad chose to be away from family and the humdrum of human problems. He sighed deeply and let his conscious mind convince his subconscious mind. Just then, a big wave came across the boat and chose to soak him. Jay was unprepared, so he gasped for a breath with closed eyes. At that moment in time, the mind was making a conscious decision to take a look at his deep-rooted desire but chose to work together with the subconscious mind to create the life he wanted.

The conscious and subconscious mind intersected, and unknowingly, he traveled thousands of miles. He was moving at light speed since he was observing the change of landscapes from islands to coastal to densely forested lands to tropical rainforests to mountains to agricultural landscapes in microseconds. He gasped for breath at this sudden transition while continuing to keep his eyes closed. Then, his eyebrows twitched as he was trying hard to concentrate on someone who resembled him except that he was bald, had a long gray beard and was dressed in an orange robe. His face was glowing as if someone had focused a LED lamp on him. Jay's mind was analyzing this person from all the angles as he was awake at the wee hours of the morning and praying with conjoined hands. He was accompanied by two other men in similar robes. They were chanting something in unison and with devotion as their vibes could be felt. Soon, these three were toiling the grounds, and he could see this man, in particular, was giving out grunting noises because of his old age, but he continued to work with his bare hands and helped his associates collect the harvest into small jute bags.

Soon, the sun set, and these three freshened up with a shared toilet. With their produce, they walked toward a village with the bags and an empty steel bowl in their hands. He observed this figure at first walking with a couple of limps, but soon his walk was energetic, and his steps were frisky even though he was wearing flat footwear, and the soles of his feet were cracked, leaving Jay very confused. They kept their bags under a tree while going from house to house seeking food for their respective empty bowls. The trio sat under a tree diagonal to where they had placed the jute bags, and before eating the donated food, they noticed how the inhabitants had collected around that tree and were distributing the produce consisting of cauliflower, cucumbers, and onions to each other while praising the Lord and them. Filled with gratitude, these three men who were sitting under a banyan tree offered their prayers and started to eat from their respective bowls.

Jay peeked in this particular man's bowl and saw the contents. It had half a slice of bread along with a few spoonfuls of rice with curry. He was done eating in a few minutes given the limited amount of food in his bowl. He then got up to pour water in his bowl from a nearby tap, swirled and drank it. He had such a content look on his face as if he had had a three-course meal. Jay was speechless, but his mind chose to hang around there. This certain man walked back to where he had started from and chose to pick up a sling bag and sit under a tree. He sat with a book reading some scriptures loudly while pausing now and then pondering over their words and making notes of them in his notebook.

Time ticked by while Jay chose to be around and assess the surroundings that were meager yet spoke of complacency. The sun was now over their heads, and the trio signaled each other who were sitting under various trees to gather their empty bowls. They went to another village that was quite a walk asking for food, and just then a random stranger came and gave Jay's look-a-like some cash. He thanked him with a bow and then shared it with his other orange-robed men. The three went to a shop where each purchased according to their needs. Jay was quick to peek into their hands and saw a bar of soap, toothpaste, a notebook, pen, and a couple of other random things. Just then, he saw this look-a-like ask for a telephone, and he dialed a number. Jay was curious to know who was on the other end. He observed this man quickly put down the receiver without talking, which was followed by deep sighs with closed, moist eyes and a content smile.

After lunch, the three walked back to their room to rest on a bare, cemented floor with a meager sheet under and over them. The pillows they used to rest their head on were a bundle of rolled-up jute. Jay observed three men shared the room, and they had occupied three walls of the room as they had their personal stuff laid up against their respective walls. All had scant belongings as he could only observe a bundle and a laid-out sheet which they would call their bed, yet he was surprised that the vibes in the room were filled with gratitude and fulfillment. At that junction, his mind and heart felt a connection since he too had the same feeling when he was packing before boarding the boat for the island.

The room was located in the middle of a fertile ground where he could see many crops growing while some had been harvested and were in jute bags. Thanks to spending life on the island, he could name them all—wheat, rice, and lentils. Soon, the men woke up, and this man, in particular, after having a glass of water from a nearby pot, went toward a tree with a sling bag outside their room and sat under the tree. Time ticked by, and Jay could see the sun set. The three men went with their empty bowls asking for food from one doorstep to another, and thereafter, they called it a night.

Just then, Mack tapped on Jay's shoulder while Yogi gave out a big slurp on his master's face. Jay was quick to open his eyes, which seemed droopy. He nodded his head in dismay to understand his surroundings, then stared at Mack. After a pause, he was quick to tell him all. "Was it a delusion or was it my future?" he asked in a very confused tone.

Mack was still contemplating and then was quick to query, "Since you kept mulling over your dad, maybe you got an opportunity to get a quick glance of his life."

"But... but," said a confused Jay trying to find the exact words. "I'm just a common man. How could I get those powers to travel miles via my mind?"

"Yes, a common man we all are, but this man when detached from everything, churns a powerful source within. That source helps channelize the subconscious mind, which if subjective, will merely execute the commands given by the conscious mind."

"Huh?"

"Your conscious mind commands, and your subconscious mind obeys," Mack said simply.

Jay was on a rollercoaster of emotions. He was at peace with what he saw but also filled with pride for his dad, who chose a difficult path in life despite all the comforts at home. He could relate to many instances since he got to live a bare-minimum kind of life on the island thanks to the shipwreck. However, he used to eat like a king while his dad was begging for food in spite of toiling on the fertile grounds and producing a yield that he and his men chose to donate to the villagers. That was followed by resentment within him for his selfish behavior all these years where his mom continued to be his caretaker while his heart was cold.

Then he felt a warm gush of affection toward his mom, who was always the light of his life beside him in spite of his choices that mostly included shunning her away. He felt foolish and an idiot for forming a shield against her, while all she did was continue to love and look out for him even during his nightmares!

His broken heart over the years was healed, and his eyes that were once icy were now sparkling with warmth, courtesy of this trip. He was keen to embrace his present and respond to the love and affection that his mom and grandparents had been pouring over him ever since his dad left. They regarded him as their sunshine, but he chose to shun them from his life. The guilt was burning him from within as he contemplated over their reactions at the thought of him approaching them with wide arms. But then, he knew that family is all about forgiveness and embraces and never has an expiry date for affection, making him very eager to reunite with them.

# CHAPTER THIRTY

*"Do not let your past hold you back from what you think you can achieve in the future."*
— **Idowu Koyenikan**


The cruise line had been contacted, and the search had started. Little did they know that the lion would come to the hunter by itself. Pictures of Jay were circulating on the island and upon his arrival, he was quickly recognized and the manhunt ended sooner than it had started. Within a day, a ticket was booked for Jay and Yogi to fly to their home on a chartered plane.

Mack insisted he buy him new clothes, but Jay was adamant to travel in that attire. He went to say goodbye and thank you to Maya and her family since courtesy of her, he got to unfold a piece off his past—Sasha. Before boarding the flight, Jay wanted some last words of advice from Mack, especially since he knew he would not be connected to him even via technology once he got back home.

"Can I visit you sometime?" asked Jay with a lump in his throat, dreading what would be the response.

"My island is not on the maps since it does not have a name and is not a tourist spot." Mack was very frank, then after a pause, "Only if you ever get shipwrecked, and destiny floats you in our direction," which pierced Jay's heart. Then, after a deep breath, he realized that this tribe was not attached to anyone even though they loved all, but their love was to set everyone free and not bind them in any way. He nodded in affirmation. "Any last words for me?" he asked with a curious smile.

"Look out for the man in your reflection."

Jay was astounded by those words. He hugged Mack. "Thank you for being my wake-up call and making me realize what all I was losing out on in life."

Mack took a while to understand the analogy. He chuckled. "Glad I could bring you back from your slumber, my friend, before it was too late. Although I was just the channel, the source was the universe."

Jay, with moist eyes, walked to the airstrip with Yogi in his hands straining to look ahead because he knew if he turned around, he would become feeble in his knees. The flight back home was filled with enthusiasm. He wanted to meet Gina, and this time he longed for his mom and his grandparents while his heart went out for his dad, feeling extremely proud of his bold choice. He was appalled for doubting him, but then came to peace when he thanked destiny for this holiday-cruise shipwreck, which was a game-changer in his life.

Minutes ticked into hours, and soon the chartered plane was landing at the San Jose International Airport strip. As he got down with Yogi in his hands, he looked around and felt at home with the surroundings. He walked along when he heard his name. Frowning at first, he tried to adjust to the brightness of the day by squinting only to see four figures standing at a distance. He raced toward them even though his mind was still a second behind, thinking *Should I?* or *Shouldn't I?*

The body ached for that familiar hug, and the heart complied with his wishes making him reach out to his grandparents and mom with open arms that were followed by an embrace, which was full of warmth and affection and fondness as he went down memory lane with each one of them. Moist eyes, wrinkled bodies, and shaky legs did not deter his mom and grandparents from continuing to hold him in that position until he let go of each of them. Gina was patiently waiting her turn, and when it came, she was quick to give him a one-arm hug with a few cuss words that were exchanged freely by both of them while the adults looked in bewilderment and moist eyes. Once all the formalities were over, Jay got busy caressing his long hair, although thanks to the razor, he could shave his grown hair off his chin and upper lip.

"Look at you! You look like some glorified soul who has come down from the mountains. You have a certain glow, and your eyes have so much peace and contentment in them as if you have meditated for years," Gina remarked.

Jay found the comment very flattering since he would see the same in the tribal people, though he never noticed it in himself in the reflection of the water in the pail each morning when he would wash up.

He was embarrassed at first, then blushed and quickly changed the topic while Yogi was playing with everyone. While driving home, he noticed the familiar signs, the mundane spray paintings on the walls of the freeways, the greenery that used to be considered as usual, but today he found it unusual and special. He had a smile for everything he was observing. There was gratitude within to be back to a place where he made all his memories. Today, as he was driving by, it struck him how much joy he got from them, but since he was enveloped in his past, he had failed to recognize it, until now.

"Café first? Right?" Gina inquired as she was about to take the exit.

"Nah, it's Christmas. Let's go home," Jay said in a very casual tone, which made Gina sneer.

"Are you all right?" she asked.

"Never been better," he said with a twinkle in his eyes. "I bet even your research would have gotten sidelined by the latter statement, huh?"

Gina paused for a bit, then after giving him a side-glance, "Oh, Jay, I did not open my research book ever since I got the news of you missing." Her tone was disheartening, and it created a sullen environment in the vehicle.

Jay was quick to break it. "Is Sam at the store?"

"Aha!" Gina said as she eyed him from the rearview mirror.

"Ask him to shut down the café and come for a meal at our home. He deserves it."

Gina's heart fluttered upon hearing it, and she gave out a wide smile. In Jay's absence, Sam and Gina had formed a special and intimate bond, and she was guilty of it. She thought she had to be mourning his absence and not be indulging in pleasure. Blushing at first, she quickly handed her phone over to him.

As Gina entered the street of his home, he noticed the red ribbons on the trees. There were lights on all the entryways, some even had a snow globe, the reindeer, Santa and his elves. Jay was looking at them with childlike eyes and chuckled, pointing at those inflated figures with sheer joy.

They entered his home, which felt like heaven for him. The living room was decorated with a Christmas tree, lights, and red poinsettias everywhere. In lieu of Jay's arrival came the desire to decorate. He gave out a loud cheer at first, and that was followed by a shriek of tears. He let them roll by. All four were taken aback at first, but then allowed him to express his heart. He sat on the couch while feeling it continuously and mumbling now and then. The four adults found it very amusing.

Mom and Gina had set up the table for a Christmas feast. "Aunt Cee-Cee will also be joining us," Mom declared to which Jay at first was shocked that they had identified her, but then he let destiny roll out the carpet so that all could embrace each other as is.

He went to his room and stared at everything. He wanted to take a shower, but he stood with his wardrobe wide open. *So many clothes while I could survive with two outfits for the last month or two. Sigh! The wants and needs of man are so mysterious.*

When he entered his restroom, he realized it sure was a room to rest with warm, flowing water, lather-rich conditioners, and fragrant soap. He was shocked at how he had taken all this for granted. *I guess the mind was churning with so many thoughts that my present was taken for granted.*

At first, he chose to wear his best attire, especially it being his favorite holiday since he had come to the United States, but instead, he found himself thinking, *what would Mack do?*

His hand straightaway looked for his comfy sweatshirt and sweatpants. He loved the soft cotton within as if somebody was hugging him and appreciated the warmth and snug feeling he got from them. When he entered the living room, Christmas carols playing in the background, and the six people seated at the table were taken aback by what he wore but chose to keep quiet. Sam approached him and hugged him for a good few minutes while Aunt Cee-Cee waited patiently for her turn.

"Welcome back!"

He peeped at the table that had half a dozen food dishes laid out. The aroma was filling the small room, which led to his stomach growling while his heart was filled with gratitude for being able to stand at this junction in his life.

He went up to his granddad and massaged his shoulders just as he used to do as a teen. He spoke some kind words to him while his heart went out to him, especially since he could understand his feelings as a father losing his son to find salvation. He hugged his grandma by her shoulders and tried to connect with her and then went and sat next to his mom. Hugging her, he inquired in a caring tone, "How have you been, Mom?"

Usha's eyes got moist, and her facial expressions were such that said, "Now, you ask?" But instead, she chose to gulp down the sarcasm and anger, shrugging her shoulders indicating that life is fine. Jay could sense her response, so he apologized upfront. "I have not been a good son. I was not there for you, especially when Dad left. I was insensitive to your needs, and honestly, I also made you responsible for him leaving us."

That last statement was kind of harsh for his mom since she glared at him for a good ten seconds then got a hold of herself and chuckled. "That's all right, son, as long as you now realize your shortcomings. Although you do realize I was the most impacted by your dad leaving. You found your company in Gina. I was left alone with no one by my side. However, your dad made sure I was trained and surrounded with work, leaving me with no time to yearn for any human company. Then even my sister, my confidante, left me while I mourned her loss alone," she said in a bitter tone, patting his hand and taking a sip of water.

Cee-Cee was quick to get up from her chair and place her hand over her shoulder, patting gently. "Usha, I hope you can forgive me. Please try to understand where I was going with it. I did not want anybody's sympathy."

Usha placed her hand over hers and nodded while sniffing silently.

Jay felt self-centered and in an apologetic tone, said, "I wish I could bring back those years so that I could be a good son to you." Then with admiration, "Mom, I'm proud of you, though. The company is doing remarkably well. You did justice to the time spent with it."

To that, everyone was quick to nod. Mom looked at them and waited for the compliments to subside, then in a very honest tone, "When your dad left me, there was anger, sorrow, regret, and self-doubt within me. But when I started to work, I got lots of encouragement, hope, love, kindness, empathy, and faith from your grandparents and the workers in the company. I chose to take that and erase the latter."

Jay was quick to hug her, and with moist eyes, he said, "Mom, I am so proud of you."

She smiled.

After a pause, he questioned, "Have you heard from Dad?" His upfront query, especially after the vision he had, made his all the more curious. He wanted more answers in particular to that phone call his dad made. On listening to him, everyone at the table became quiet. It was a subject that was considered taboo, especially since it had left a scar on everyone's heart.

Granddad broke the silence by clearing his throat. Grandma showed no resistance in controlling her sobs. Usha, on the other hand, pinched herself hard to avoid that tear from trickling down, while Gina, Sam, and Cee-Cee had nothing to contribute but just be the audience.

Seeing the resistance, Jay clarified, "Yes, I know this has always been a taboo topic in our household, but more because we miss him. But, why don't we try to be proud of his actions since living such a lifestyle is not easy."

Eyes stared at him with frowns to which he went on to explain his life after the shipwreck. He talked about the island, and the newborn named after his dad. And he also talked about Mack, his sole English-speaking partner who made him get rid of all his hiccups of his past, including Sasha. At the end, everyone was blown away, but that was also followed by many questions.

Mom, after quickly glancing to her in-laws, said, "Yes, we do hear from him now and then. I get missed calls from one particular number." She chuckled, wiping her tears.

"What's the use of that?" Gina interrupted in a scoffing tone.

"I guess love makes him want to do that, but at the same time, he draws a line by being unattached to all of us."

While they continued to devour the chicken roast with cranberry and mango chutney and the freshly baked crescents and house salad, they also had a moment to ponder upon Jay's first few words of wisdom.

"Mom, I visited him."

There was pin-drop silence as all just stared at him with either their mouths full or empty.

Then he clarified, "I had a vision."

"You mean you dreamed of him in your sleep?" Grandma inquired then went on, "I, too, dream of him a lot." And then she continued to sob quietly.

"No, Grandma. I actually saw his lifestyle. I even saw him dial you, Mom, but since I did not hear the other end, I was not sure, so I thought of inquiring."

That left all at the table very confused. Mom got concerned. "I think the island where you were marooned had some magical powers over you. You should take it easy."

Gina could partially understand what he was going at but chose to be quiet. Aunt Cee-Cee changed the topic by praising the mango chutney.

Jay was insistent. "Mom, do you know his whereabouts?"

"I got it back-tracked to a village in the north of Himachal Pradesh. I guess when he comes to the village to shop for his basic needs, he gives us a missed call."

"Did you ever talk to him?"

She went silent, then with moist eyes, she admitted, "I have never heard his voice since he left our home. Although he makes sure he hears mine, and then he hangs up." Then after a pause, "He is so selfish," she confessed with tears.

Surprisingly, Jay was open to accepting the comment. "Had he been thinking of only himself, those calls would never come, Mom."

That broke Mom down. "You have come a full circle, son."

********

With Christmas lunch out of the way, Sam inquired if they should continue with the tradition of him being the Santa in the café to which Jay immediately nodded. They all went to the café decorated in normal Christmas tradition. It had wreaths, a small Christmas tree, and candy canes all over the place, just as Jay would decorate each year. It brought a smile to his face as he admired them all. Gina brought out the books to show him his profits while Jay immediately placed a hand over it and pushed them away, "I trust you. The café is in one piece. What more can I ask?"

he said with a smile filled with gratitude.

She was shocked. Sam went to change into his Santa attire and was soon sitting on a red chair while Gina was dressed as his elf. She brought out the eats that consisted of strawberry Santa cupcakes with red and white frosting, peanut-butter cup Christmas trees, and Christmas cookies from the refrigerator and placed them out for sale. Jay glanced at them and was surprised at her creativity. She blushed and confessed that she had baked them on Christmas Eve.

Mom, Cee-Cee, and the grandparents were sipping their favorite tea in the corner of the café when the kids and their parents entered to which Gina, the elf, rings the bell. After listening to every story each child had to narrate, Santa handed them a candy cane and then asked them to rush to the counter to purchase goodies. Jay was at the counter. Suddenly, something caught Gina's ear. It was the register. It was not clicking, and the children were running out with their baked goodies in their hands. She turned around to see that Jay was giving it all away for free!

Her eyes were left wide open as if she had had a shot of whiskey. She nudged her Santa, who stopped interacting with the kid on his lap and was equally stunned. Jay noticed the expressions on the elf and Santa's face and winked back.

Sam twitched his eyebrows while Gina murmured, "Praise for Mack, the tutor who helped relieve his hiccup of years, and through magical realism, he got a chance to visit his past helping him come to peace with it. This helped him listen to the call of love, both from his loved ones and also from his own heart. He finally reciprocated to all the love that he was surrounded with." Then after a pause, "And it all helped me complete my research work on this tough subject with a guaranteed Masters' degree!"

She winked while giving out a crooked smile.
**THE END**